JAKE

Ingram Brothers #2

ROZ LEE

ISBN-13:978-1-966224-10-5

Ingram Brothers #
JAKE
USA TODAY BESTSELLING AUTHOR
ROZ LEE

DEDICATION

For my wonderful readers who encourage me to tell my stories.

CHAPTER ONE

Jake Ingram paced the confines of his office. He'd changed nothing, not the ugly carpet, not the heavy oak desk, not a picture or a book on the massive library shelves taking up one entire wall, since the day he'd stepped in to take over his father's mediocre law practice nearly a decade ago.

He wanted out. Not only out of the office. Out of the stagnant life he'd made for himself. Despite never wanting to be a lawyer, he was good at what he did. He helped people and made a decent living at it. But, on days like today, these four walls were a prison he couldn't escape. The large picture window looking out on a well-maintained courtyard behind the building should have provided solace, but, instead, it reminded him of a zoo enclosure, but he was on the wrong side of the glass.

He stopped his pacing to watch a squirrel dart around the lawn, grabbing up whatever it could find in the way of food. He understood the rodent's anxiety. Jake's belly was full, but he couldn't shake the emptiness inside.

These feelings weren't new. He'd recognized them long ago and successfully shoved them aside—until now. Ever since he'd laid eyes on the self-portrait his brother Will painted, the hollow pit in his gut had grown wider and deeper.

He closed his eyes against the hot sun beating down on the courtyard, and Will's painting immediately came to mind. It consisted of three enormous canvases he'd hung from the joists in their other brother, Rick's, garage. Each panel, covered with splashes of color, represented different facets of his brother—or so Will claimed. Will Ingram was a broken man, evidenced by the violent way he'd slung the paint—as if he'd dug into his soul with his bare hands and flung the ugliness away.

He'd pretended confusion at what Rick deemed a mess in his garage, but Jake instantly recognized the pain behind the painting. Staring at the slashes of black and red had been like looking in a mirror. He didn't know what hurt more, seeing his own unhappiness, his lack of fulfillment hanging there for all to see, or discovering the depth of his brother's despair matched his own.

He swallowed a groan then rubbed his palms over his face and turned toward his desk and the note his admin left for him. The private investigator he'd hired to look for the lowlifes who'd stolen Will's paintings had called. He closed the mental door on his own misery and focused on his brother's case. Since baring his soul in the painting, Will was in a better frame of mind these days. He'd opened up about his ordeal in New York, how he'd been duped by Jessica Blackwell, his fiancée/agent, and the gallery owner, Cecil Hawthorne, she'd secretly been sleeping with. Between the two of them, they'd emptied his bank accounts and made off with close to a million dollars' worth of Will's canvases.

Jake managed to recover most of his brother's cash by convincing the banker his employee had made a huge mistake by turning the funds over to someone who wasn't signatory on the account. Faced with the facts, he'd opted to replace the lost money. His brother said the paintings didn't matter, and maybe they didn't to the new Will Ingram, but Jake knew in his gut, sooner or later, the canvases would surface in the future. He wanted to find them and the people who'd snatched them before the culprits struck again. His brothers were all the family he had left, and he'd do anything to protect them.

Still too agitated to sit, he picked up the phone and dialed the private detective's number.

❧

Jake waved and smiled at the TSA agent guarding the funnel from the gates to baggage claim at New York's JFK airport. The guy probably was calling for backup now, but he didn't care. He wasn't in Willowbrook, and he was going to take full advantage of this rare opportunity to breathe.

He loved his hometown, and he loved his brothers, Will and Rick, but he'd never planned on spending his entire adult life living in someone else's shoes.

He located the car and driver he'd hired waiting for him outside baggage claim and followed the man out into the humidity. Texas could be a bitch in the summer, but New York won the misery contest, hands down. He aimed to be in the city for a day or two then he was heading upstate where he hoped the hunting and the weather would be better. His prey had long since left town. Manhattan was big, but it was also expensive. Plus, why risk being seen by friends or old associates? It made more sense for the thieves to skedaddle, to lie low until their trail grew cold and it was safe to put the next phase of their plan into action. He suspected the culprits planned to ransom Will's paintings back to him—otherwise, why not destroy them at the gallery?

Which brought up another question. How did they transport all those canvases? It was a question he'd asked his private investigator to look into and hoped the answer would provide a solid lead.

Jake checked into his hotel then walked the few blocks to the private detective's midtown office. The small office occupied space in a century-old building but was, nonetheless, neat and well-kept. While he waited for his appointment, he studied the colorful nature photographs adorning the reception area walls. He'd hired Philip Holland on the recommendation of a friend from law school, and, so far, he hadn't been disappointed. His work was thorough and often went beyond Jake's expectations, and though he'd talked with the investigator on multiple occasions, he was looking forward to meeting him in person.

At the sound of heavy footsteps approaching, he turned. Philip Holland looked exactly as Jake had pictured him. Standing just under six feet with a slight paunch, the former NYPD detective who'd put in his twenty years before retiring to open his own business wore a brown, off-the-rack suit, a beige dress shirt, and a patterned tie Jake estimated to be older than he was. Lines deeply engraved around his eyes and lips spoke of years of cigarette use and things seen but not forgotten. With his thinning hair and scuffed brown dress shoes he'd blend into any crowd. "Mr. Ingram, I presume."

"Jake, please. You must be Mr. Holland." He extended his arm and they shook hands.

"You can call me Philip. It's a pleasure to meet you." He spoke to his receptionist. "If Sanderson calls, put him through. Otherwise, take a message."

Holland's office was as neat and stylish as the public space. Where the reception area had hardwood flooring, the boss's office boasted plush carpeting and a wall of windows overlooking the busy street below. The investigator took a seat behind his contemporary, industrial-chic style desk, waving Jake to a worn leather chair facing him.

They discussed Jake's trip and complained about the weather before the PI opened a file and got down to business. "You asked me to look into several things for you. Have you changed your mind about any of them?"

He appreciated the man's discretion, but he'd made up his mind. "No. This is my brother's livelihood, and possibly his life, we're talking about. I can't afford to assume anything about anyone involved."

"Okay, then." He sat forward and put on a pair of black-rimmed reading glasses. "I don't think there's anything new to report on Cecil Hawthorne's former PR woman, MacKenzie Carlysle. She never lied about who she was, and any cover-up of her involvement appears to have been her father's doing, not hers. Everyone I spoke with said the same thing—she's honest and hardworking. She's never used her father's influence to obtain a job or social status. What little she has, she's worked for."

"Her ending up in Willowbrook was coincidence?"

"As far as I can see, yes. When she left New York, she was practically penniless. Her bank account didn't have enough in it to pay the monthly service fee, and she was charging everything to a credit card she'd had for years and rarely used. She'd been living in a friend's apartment, sleeping on a cot in the closet, until another friend, Sunny Sheldon, helped her find the job in Texas. Her current employer paid for her plane ticket to Dallas; otherwise, she would have been hitchhiking."

"She didn't go to her father for help?"

"I couldn't find any evidence she asked him for assistance. Her roommate said MacKenzie and her father had an ongoing disagreement about her decision not to go to law school. According to her, they hadn't spoken in years."

"But he intervened on her behalf with the NYPD."

"The lead investigator, Detective Reeves, mentioned her father made some calls. In the detective's defense, he said the girl was so squeaky clean he saw no reason to look any closer at her."

After what his brother told him about the way he and MacKenzie met, the way she ended up in Willowbrook at the same time had raised questions in Jake's mind—and Will's, too. It was a relief to know she'd been telling the truth about her lack of involvement in the theft. "When I talked to her, she seemed genuine in her desire to help. She was the one who gave me the lead about Ross McClelland."

"Speaking of." He shuffled the papers in the file. "I think we've located him. My associate, Mike Sanderson, is checking into it as we speak. If it is him, he lives in Callicoon, a tiny little community up in the Catskills. I can have Sanderson question him if you like."

Jake shook his head. "I'd prefer to do it myself, unless you think he's dangerous?"

"I doubt it. He's seventy-five years old and in failing health."

"I'll go talk to him, see if he knows anything we can use to track down Hawthorne."

Holland turned the McClelland report facedown then picked up another one. "We also located the real estate agent your brother and his former fiancée, Jessica Blackwell spoke to. Sanderson didn't question the woman, per your request."

"I'll talk to her, too."

"Let me remind you, these individuals could be dangerous. If you get too close, no telling what they might do to protect their secrets."

"I understand. If I find Hawthorne and Blackwell, or get even the slightest hint of danger, I'll get the police involved."

"Sanderson is available if you want company."

"I don't plan to go alone." Unless the PI's final report changed his mind.

"Good to know." He set aside the real estate agent's file and picked up another. "That brings us to your final inquiry, Sunny Sheldon."

At the mention of the gallery owner, Jake's entire body responded. He'd met her briefly the last time he'd come to the city. There'd been a spark between them, but, at the time, she'd been on his list of suspects, potential accomplices in the disappearance of his brother's paintings. He'd had plenty of experience with liars and knew you couldn't always rely on your ability to ferret one out. Sometimes, you needed to dig deeper to locate the deceit. So, he'd added Sunny to the investigator's list. He nodded for the man to continue.

"Most everything about Ms. Sheldon is public knowledge. Her father is Curtis Sheldon, the actor. She grew up in the public eye, at her father's side for most of the major accomplishments in his life. Her parents divorced when she was a baby, but they shared custody. Her mother is from a well-known New York family and currently resides in Los Angeles. Ms. Sheldon inherited a great deal of money from her maternal grandmother, as well as a historic brownstone here in the city. She's lived independently since she was eighteen. Bought what is now Sunnyside Gallery, when she was twenty-one. Never been married. Dates occasionally but has never been involved in any kind of scandal, celebrity or otherwise. Never done drugs. Doesn't drink to excess. Stays to herself, except for attending gallery openings and charity events. She still does the occasional red-carpet event with her father. When she is confronted by paparazzi, she lets them take a few photos then moves on. Therefore, there are lots of pictures of her which makes them virtually worthless to someone who makes a living selling celeb photos."

"Any hint of a relationship with Cecil Hawthorne or Jessica Blackwell?"

"None. She knows them. Everyone in the art world does, but like everybody else we talked to, they were acquaintances, not friends."

"Cecil and Jessica didn't have any friends in the industry?"

"I didn't find any. They kept to themselves. It's not unheard of in this city. Acquaintances and associates are easy to come by. Friends, not so much. MacKenzie Carlysle and Sunny Sheldon are exceptions to the rule. They both have a lot of friends who sing their praises."

Jake nodded. "Got anything else?"

"Not at this time. Sanderson hasn't called. I'll let you know when I hear from him. I'm 99 percent certain the guy in Callicoon is our man, but there's no use going all the way out there if it turns out he's not." He arranged all the papers back in the folder then slid it across the desk. "These are your copies."

He took the folder and stood. The two men shook hands. "Thanks for all your hard work."

"All in a day's work."

The heat out on the sidewalk made him wish he'd called the car service again, but the walk to his hotel was a short one. Entering the lobby, he made a beeline for the bar where he ordered a cold beer and drank it while reading through the reports Philip had compiled. He skimmed the ones on top, eager to get to the last one.

Sunny Sheldon had occupied his thoughts and his dreams since the first moment he'd seen her. On his previous trip to the Big Apple to straighten out Will's finances, he'd stopped by her gallery to ask her some questions. If he'd been a celebrity follower, he probably would have recognized her. But he didn't have time for frivolous things, hardly watched TV, and couldn't recall the last time he'd been to a movie theater. When she'd invited him to her office for tea, the photos of her and her father scattered around her private space revealed her identity.

He'd been attracted to her from the start, but her celebrity status and her friendship with MacKenzie Carlysle made him reluctant to ask her out. Thus, the report. He didn't desire fame, or infamy, and he sure didn't need to complicate his brother's situation by getting involved with a potential suspect.

Will had assured him the gallery owner wasn't involved, and Jake had thought the same after talking to her. The inquiry was a safety measure because she tripped wires in his brain, and he didn't trust himself to make a rational decision where she was concerned. If he was seriously considering asking her to accompany him on his trip upstate, then it had been way too long since he'd been with a woman.

CHAPTER TWO

Sunny paced the gallery floor, devoid of customers on this hot, sticky summer day. She should have closed shop and gone out to the Hamptons like every other New Yorker and left the steamy streets to the tourists. She'd put off the trip because *he* might come back. Jake Ingram.

Only an idiot spent her days wishing a man would call, and her nights wishing she'd tried harder to get the sexy Texan in her bed when she'd had the chance.

She hadn't seen or heard from him in a month.

If his disappearing act didn't scream not interested, nothing did.

Yet, here she sat, bored and pining for someone who probably forgot she existed the minute he walked out the door of her gallery.

He'd said he would return.

And like a fool, she'd believed him. She'd waited for a call saying he was on the way.

He'd pledged to return, but his eyes vowed so much more. The unspoken promise of sex hot enough to set off the fire alarm kept her awake at night, wondering what his hands and lips would feel like on her skin. Wondering if making love with a man like him would live up to her imagination. There wasn't anything metrosexual about him. No fancy hair gel. No manicures, and she guessed, no manscaping. He made no excuses for being a man.

The long, tall Texan wasn't anything like the men she met in New York. They were all so polite, so afraid they'd be accused of sexual harassment if they showed any genuine interest. They'd never look at her like a starving man with her the last pastry on the planet. Only Jake Ingram had ever done so.

No, there was nothing wishy-washy about Jake. The man exuded alpha-male confidence from the crown of his dark head to the tips of his western boots.

He'd be the kind to take control in the bedroom, like he did in the courtroom. Yeah, sue her. She'd googled him, all the while hoping he hadn't done the same to her. He already knew about her famous father, and perhaps her minor celebrity status had scared him away. No guy wanted to end up on the cover of a tabloid because they dated the wrong woman. If he'd given her a chance, she could have explained. The paparazzi didn't care about her unless she did something with her dad or for a charity. Boring didn't sell papers, and her life defined boredom. He had nothing to fear.

But he'd never given her the chance to tell him. He'd gone home to Texas, leaving her with more fantasies than she knew what to do with. She spent way too much time daydreaming about a man who, despite his promise to return, had probably forgotten all about her the second he'd left .

"Enough!" Sunny verbally scolded herself then stomped off to her office. It was time to stop acting like a lovesick teenager and get on with her life. Jake went home where he probably had a stable of fillies eager to give him a ride whenever the mood struck. The Texan wasn't the kind of man who did without or who saw to his own needs.

She took a minute to call the garage where she stored her car then powered the computer system down and grabbed her purse. She'd go home, pack a bag, and go to the beach. She checked the lock on the back door then turned out lights as she made her way to the front of the shop. What remained of the daylight and the spotlights trained on the window display provided ample illumination. She stopped for a moment to turn off the lamp on the front desk when movement outside the front window caught her attention.

A customer, perhaps. Her only one today and reason to wait a few moments to see. Edging closer, she peeked out the window. Her heart skipped a beat.

She blinked then took another peek. Her mind wasn't playing tricks on her. Jake Ingram had returned. Deferring to the heat, he'd left off his suit coat and rolled up the sleeves of his dress shirt to reveal muscular forearms as he stood on the sidewalk, eyes downcast, hands stuffed in the pockets of his light-gray dress slacks. He looked good enough to eat.

Her heart tumbled. Was this a business call and he was choosing his words carefully to catch her in a lie? She had nothing more to add to her statement. She'd told him everything. She'd done her best to help him and his brother. She genuinely liked Will Ingram and hoped he was painting again. She'd take anything he wanted to sell. His older brother, however, was another story. He seemed to be the opposite of the well-known painter, yet she was drawn to him. Wanted to get to know him better.

Gritting her teeth against the bitter disappointment brewing in her gut, she crossed to the door and jerked it open. "Are you going to stand here all day, or are you coming in?"

Jake's chin rose, and the expressive eyes etched into her memory from a month ago met hers. The smile breaking across his face incinerated her anger. "I was waiting for you. I saw the lights go out, figured you were closing early, so I waited." He took a step forward. "Didn't want to spook you by coming in."

"Spook me?" New Yorkers didn't spook people. They scared the shit out of them, but spook? No. "Is that Texan for give me a heart attack?"

"You know it, darlin'." His gaze swept past her to the darkened and deserted shop. "Everyone gone for the day?"

"It's just me today. It's too hot for people to be out shopping."

"I won't argue with you. It is hot out here. Looks cooler in there." He nodded to the interior of the shop.

"Would you like to come in?"

"Don't mind if I do."

She turned the Open sign to Closed and threw the dead bolt. They stood facing each other, ambient light from the street and the window spotlights casting shadows over their features.

"Give me a second. I'll turn on some lights."

"No need. I didn't come to see the artwork."

"What did you come for, Jake?"

He gave the place a cursory glance then his gaze landed on her, and, with a little huff of breath, he confessed, "I don't have the faintest idea." He gave her his back. One strong hand kneaded the nape of his neck. This wasn't the same confident, bordering-on-arrogant man she'd met months ago. What had made him this indecisive?

"Are you here on business?" she prompted. "Did you find your brother's paintings?" If he'd recovered them, she'd do whatever it took to consign some. W.H. Ingram's paintings always sold well in her shop.

At her questions, Jake faced her, shaking his head. "I haven't found the paintings, but I have a couple of leads. I need to go upstate, chase a few people down who might have answers." He glanced at the floor then lifted his gaze to hers. "I could use some company." His lips quirked up on one corner. "Want to ride along?"

Sunny's jaw dropped. Surely, she'd misheard. "You want me to go with you?"

He nodded, and she glimpsed the banked heat in his eyes. So maybe all the sexy dreams she'd had about him weren't as one-sided as she'd thought. Upstate could be as miserable, weather-wise, as the city, but if the company was good, a woman might overlook a few inconveniences. "How long will you be gone?"

"Don't know. A few days? A week?"

She could call Ginger. Ask her to open the shop a few hours a day while she was gone. "Where're you going?"

"Not a clue."

"Then you'll need a guide." She hadn't spent much time upstate, but her dad owned a house in Westchester. Getting there and back without getting lost wouldn't be a problem.

"Yeah. I guess I will. You up for the job?"

Her heart raced as she pretended to consider his offer, when she didn't care where he was going as long as he wanted her along. It had been way too long since she'd experienced the intense attraction Jake inspired. She'd watched him walk away once. She had no intention of letting it happen again. "I'm in." She picked up her purse from where she'd left it on the desk. "When do we leave?"

Jake followed her. "Tomorrow?"

Sunny opened the door, ushered Jake to the sidewalk, then locked the door. "How about tonight? I can be ready in an hour."

Sunny studied the man behind the Jeep's wheel. She'd never seen Jake in anything but a suit and took in his "casual" attire—worn jeans, a crisp white button-down shirt, sleeves rolled up to reveal strongly muscled forearms. The man was gorgeous. The cowboy boots were sexy as hell, too.

"Where are we going?"

"New Castle. Will and Jessica stopped there once, inquired about some land for sale."

"You think Jessica and Cecil are in the area?"

"I don't know. Maybe. It's a place to start."

Sunny took in the passing scenery. She rarely left Manhattan. When she did, she usually went to her dad's house in the Hamptons. He used the retreat a few weeks in the summer, schedule permitting. The rest of the year, the place sat vacant. Sunny loved it, would live there year-round if the commute wasn't horrendous. The trees lining the parkway were beautiful, but having grown up in Southern California, she was more of a beach girl.

She glanced at him. "What do you think?"

"About?"

She waved her hand to indicate the scenery. "The trees. The area. Is this your kind of place?"

She caught the rise and fall of his shoulders out of the corner of her eye. "It's okay. Sort of makes me claustrophobic. Things are more open in Texas. I can see for miles from my backyard."

"Your brother wanted to buy land up here?"

"Will was looking for studio space. When he's working, it doesn't matter what's outside. Trees, fields, skyscrapers. Hell, he'd probably be happy in a lighthouse perched on a rock in the middle of the ocean."

"He's that focused?"

"He used to be. After…this, I'm not so sure. He hasn't painted much since he came home."

"But he is painting?" She'd really hate to think one of the country's best talents walked away.

"Yeah. Some." Jake's fingers gripped the steering wheel until his knuckles shown white.

Sensing his reluctance to discuss his brother's work, she changed the subject. "I prefer the beach. I grew up in Los Angeles. Water is my thing. Pools. Lakes. Oceans."

He relaxed his hold on the wheel. "My home is on a lake. And I have a pool."

"My dad has a beach house on Long Island."

"You go there often?"

"Not as much as I would like." She shifted on the seat so she faced him. "Is it a big lake?"

"Haven't you heard? Everything in Texas is big." His sexy grin made her smile and warmed parts of her body she'd almost forgotten existed.

He'd been the perfect gentleman since he stepped into her gallery yesterday, and though she appreciated it, she wanted more. She wanted what his eyes promised. If it meant stripping his gentlemanly veneer away, she was up to the task. She dropped her gaze to his crotch. "Everything?" she asked, infusing the single word with as much faux innocence as she could muster. She'd learned a few things about acting from her dad.

He caught her watching him and adjusted his position in the bucket seat. "You aren't playing fair, Ms. Sheldon. Keep it up and we'll be pulling off, looking for a quiet place in the woods."

Teasing Jake was fun. She liked this new, more casual side of the staid lawyer. She glanced out at the passing scenery. "I'm beginning to appreciate the benefit of all this green stuff. However…" She faced forward again. "We're on a mission here. We need to focus."

"You're right, though, you could easily distract me if you wanted to."

Their gazes met for a brief second. "Is that a challenge?" she asked before Jake shifted his attention to the road.

"Maybe." They passed a semi then he checked the side-view mirror and moved back into the right-hand lane. "Did I thank you for coming with me?"

"Did I thank you for inviting me along?"

"You might have."

She swiveled her head, caught him grinning at her. The heat remained in his gaze, but he'd banked it. She silently vowed to nibble away at his control every chance she got. She smiled at him. "Well, thank you. I enjoy being with you. This is a pleasant change from the city."

His smile vanished, ending the playful moment as he reminded her why they were here. "We're probably wasting our time. There's zero evidence the culprits who stole Will's paintings came this way. For all we know, they've destroyed them."

"If they wanted to destroy them, they easily could have done so in the gallery. Slashed them. Tossed paint or turpentine on them. They didn't, so I'd wager they have other plans for them. Maybe they hope to ransom them at a later date."

"When they run out of the money they stole from him?"

"Who knows? But as a member of the same art world they inhabited, I'm confident they didn't take the paintings so they could destroy them later. They plan to sell them on the black market or ransom them back to Will. Those are the only scenarios that make sense."

He nodded. "This way, they draw the torture out," he surmised. "Steal the money and the artwork. Crush the gallery opening. Pull the rug out from under the artist then wait until he's moved on, put the incident behind him then hit him again. Ransom one or two at a time. Drag the pain out over decades."

"It's vengeance at its best, don't you think?"

"It's sadistic." Jake checked the mirrors then moved into the left lane to pass another slow-moving truck. "What could Will have ever done to warrant this kind of revenge?"

"I have no idea. I've only met your brother a few times, but he seemed like a nice guy. You remind me of him. Not just your looks, you're remarkably similar there, but in your mannerisms. You're good people, both of you."

"Which brings me back to my question. Why Will?"

"I think he ran afoul of the wrong person."

"Jessica Blackwell?"

"I met her a time or two. I'm from Hollywood, remember? Her kind were all over the place. Everything is about them. They need to be the center of attention. I can't speak to Will's relationship with her, but he'd become extremely popular in the New York art world. Like I said, he's a friendly guy. People liked him, and he has an extraordinary talent."

"I know what you mean. I came to visit him once before he met Jessica. He took me to a couple of shindigs he'd been invited to. I might as well have been wallpaper. Everyone gravitated to him. Fawned over him."

She cocked her head. "I didn't realize you'd been to parties in New York."

Jake shrugged. "It was a few years ago, and nobody paid me any mind. They came to see Will, not his no-talent brother."

"Shame I wasn't at any of those events."

"How do you know you weren't?"

"Because I would have noticed you."

His gaze swept over her, lingering on her lips, then her breasts. "I damn sure would have noticed you, too."

His heated assessment warmed her from the inside out. She needed to keep this light or, like he'd said, they'd end up shagging in the forest. "Really? What makes you think so?"

"Fuck, Sunny." His grip tightened on the steering wheel. "You're beautiful, and the sexiest woman I've ever seen. I was a goner the moment I laid eyes on you."

And there it was, the acknowledgment she wasn't imagining the attraction between them. Her blood pressure spiked, and her skin tingled. "You aren't the first man to tell me those things, but when you say them, I believe you're being truthful. You see me as sexy and beautiful."

"The others weren't sincere?"

"Nope. Flattery comes with the territory in the entertainment industry. Men have been trying to weasel their way into my panties since I sprouted breasts. You'd be surprised what guys will say to convince a woman to part her legs." She suppressed a shudder as unpleasant memories rushed forward.

"I must be doing something wrong if those things didn't sound like flattery to you." He cut his eyes toward her. "I intended them to."

"Watch where you're going, Romeo." She waited until he focused on the road again. "I know you were flattering me, but it's not only the words. It's the speaker's inflection, and the way they look at you, too."

"Are you saying my flattery is different from other's?"

She considered the many glib lines tossed her way over the years. Only one other rang true—a testament to the man's acting skills. It had all been a lie wrapped up in pretty but meaningless words. Thankfully, she'd learned the truth before the tabloids found out about their brief relationship. One thing she liked best about Jake was that he wasn't an actor. She glanced at his strong profile, admired the air of competence about him that came from knowing exactly who he was. Actors, it seemed, were always trying to find a piece of themselves in each role they played. "All I'm saying is, some of the best actors in the world have said similar things to me. With you, it's different."

CHAPTER THREE

He was swimming in some deep waters. The more Sunny talked, the more he understood how lucky he was to be in her company and how bad he would hurt her. She trusted him. Let him in when she should have slammed the door in his face. As much as he enjoyed being with her, they only had a few days together. He knew it, but he wasn't sure she did.

He risked a glance her way. Eyes closed, head tossed back to catch the breeze through the open window, she was every man's fantasy. Way out of his league, yet they were good together. Easy. Relaxed. She'd been open and honest about her feelings and her life, and he'd planned to repay her with sex and a self-serving road trip. She deserved better—yet the thought of another man touching her made him want to kill someone.

There couldn't be two more different people on the planet—yet something about her drew him. It wasn't only her looks, though he wouldn't deny her beauty. Her golden hair matched her name, and her blue eyes reminded him of the Texas sky on a summer day. He loved the snappy business suits she wore to work. They showed off her womanly figure while still retaining a prim-and-proper appearance that made him want to do decidedly improper things to her. Today's outfit—shorts and a sleeveless blouse with buttons down the front—reminded him of a teenage girl out for a day at the lake, but the clothes were no less sexy than her business suits. His fingers itched to pop those buttons, tasting every inch of her skin as it appeared.

What future could they possibly have? He lived his boring life in Texas, and she had a vibrant life here. She attended black-tie affairs with movie stars, and he ate take-out barbeque all alone while he watched rented movies starring those same people. Beauty aside, behind the face she showed the world lurked something he saw in himself. Loneliness. Restlessness? Her life seemed exciting to him, but was it as unfulfilling as his? She didn't speak of close friends or relatives. Spoke only of large, media circus events.

"I'm not keeping you from doing something with your friends this weekend, am I?" They'd driven north with plans to rent two rooms for the night then visit the real estate office his private investigator located the next day.

"No. I didn't have any plans, and if I did, I would have cancelled them." She smiled at him. "I'd rather be with you."

"What would you be doing if I hadn't shown up?"

"Laundry?" She turned to the passing scenery. "Actually, I thought about closing the gallery for a few days and getting out of town. Then I found you on the sidewalk and changed my mind."

"Where would you have gone?"

"To my dad's beach house. He's filming in L.A. for the summer, so I'd have the place to myself."

"You wouldn't have been alone for long."

"What makes you say so?"

Jake shrugged. "I don't know. A beautiful woman like you? I'm sure you attract people like flowers attract bees."

"Dad's place is pretty isolated. No one would know I was there unless I told them, and trust me, I wouldn't tell anyone."

She didn't deny the bees-to-flowers comparison. "Why not?"

"Because." She straightened in the seat. "I'm not a social

butterfly."

He was being a dick, pressing her for answers, but he wanted to know the mysterious woman accompanying him. He'd met no one like her, except maybe himself. "I bet you go out with friends in the city every weekend."

"You'd lose your bet, cowboy. I couldn't tell you the last time I went out with friends."

❦❧

Yes, she could tell him about her last date. But she didn't want to talk about Ian with Jake. She'd met Ian Reynolds when his mother and her dad starred in a Broadway production together. She'd been six or seven and Ian a year older. During the summer months, they'd spent nearly every minute backstage under the watchful eye of a hired babysitter. After that summer, they didn't see each other for years. When they met again, Ian had become an accomplished actor in his own right, and she'd recently graduated from college. They'd dated in secret for a few months. He'd said all the perfect words, and the sex, though not spectacular, filled a need. He'd convinced her to take the relationship public, albeit quietly. Dinner at an exclusive restaurant where paparazzi weren't welcome, making it a favorite for the Hollywood crowd. They'd be spotted but only by friends. People they could trust. Like the woman who approached their table, her pregnant belly leading the way, to confront Ian.

The evidence he'd been sleeping with her and the starlet at the same time was right there at eye level. Worst of all, Ian didn't deny anything. He'd known about the baby for months and had been dragging his feet on the custody and support agreement. Sunny excused herself from the conversation, hailed a cab, and decided being alone was underrated. It suited her fine, until she met Jake.

From the very first, she'd been attracted to the Texas lawyer in a way she'd never experienced with anyone else. Part of it was physical. Pheromones or some such. But the interest went deeper, for her, at least. She'd felt an unexplainable connection with him. Maybe it was his devotion to his brother or the way he'd looked at her, like she was a puzzle he wanted desperately to solve—one piece at a time. Whatever it was, the intervening weeks when she'd heard nothing from him hadn't diminished the attraction one bit. She wanted to be with this man. Wanted to feel his body pressing hers into a mattress. Wanted to feel him inside her. Wanted to trust him.

Jake was a handsome man. Not Hollywood Heartthrob handsome or rich, but those weren't qualities she valued. He did well for himself. She'd take a hardworking man any day over one who pretended to be something he wasn't. Actors made lousy spouses. As much as she loved her father, he was a perfect example to prove her point. He loved her mother, and her mother loved him. But their love, no matter how strong, couldn't hold their marriage together. According to her mom, Curtis Sheldon was impossible to live with. She often said she never knew who to expect when he walked in the door—Curtis or the character he portrayed on set. She'd warned Sunny of the duplicity she thought inherent in entertainers. Remembering her time with Ian, she realized how right her mother had been.

She shook off the unwanted memories of her failed love affair. "What about you? What do you do for fun?"

He glanced at her then back to the road. "I spend my weekends at the local honky-tonk. Line dancing and flirting with every female in sight."

Sunny laughed. "You do not."

"No. I don't." The smile he directed her way hit like a bolt of lightning, striking her at her core. "Would you believe I moonlight as a dancer in an all-male review?"

"Not in a million years." She grinned at him. With a few words, he'd chased her off the gloomy path her thoughts had taken her down and onto a now-familiar one where only the two of them existed. "Tell me the truth, Jake."

"I spend most nights and weekends alone. I get together

with my brothers occasionally now that they're both home."

"What do you and your siblings do?"

Sunny relaxed, content to let the wind whip at her hair and Jake's drawl smooth away the ragged edges of her mood. She would not let her past intrude on what little time she had with him. As soon as he wrapped up his brother's case, he'd go home to Texas for good. It's where he belonged. *And I'll stay in New York. It's where I belong.*

The unwanted reminder cut like a sharp blade.

Focus on the here and now.

The situation reminded her of several other times in her life when she'd been forced to make the most of circumstances she wished she could change. Her parents' divorce, Ian's betrayal, and the decision to move to New York and make a fresh start in the brownstone she'd inherited from her grandmother.

She'd known from the beginning Jake wouldn't be staying. Whatever this was between them, it was temporary. A good time. Friendly conversation. A much-needed road trip and great sex—she hoped. She'd be wise to remember that was all it was and not let the perfection of the moment lull her into believing it could be more.

"Sunny? You awake over there?"

"Huh?" She sat up, suddenly aware her eyes had drifted shut. "What?"

Jake chuckled. "Didn't mean to bore you to sleep."

Sunny rubbed her hands over her face. A quick glance told her they were coming into a town. Signs touting local businesses dotted the side of the road. Rows of mailboxes marked the entrance to dirt paths. She couldn't imagine living in such a remote place. "You didn't bore me. I guess I was more tired than I thought."

"I anticipated getting to know each other a little more tonight, but you need your sleep."

Was he suggesting what she thought he was? God, she hoped so. Heat rose in her cheeks. "I'm fine. Honestly. It must be all this fresh air. I'm a city girl, not used to this much oxygen." *I can sleep when you're gone.* "Besides, we have so little time together. I don't want to waste it sleeping."

His gaze left the road, locking with hers for a second. All kinds of things swirled in the depth of his gaze—heat, desire, acknowledgment, regret. The therapist she'd seen after the breakup with Ian would question if she was projecting her feelings into the moment. Even if she *was* seeing things she wanted to see, she'd never regret the time spent with Jake. Every minute was an experience to cherish, including falling asleep to the sound of his voice.

Jake returned his attention to the road. A muscle clenched in his jaw, and he shifted in his seat. "Dammit, woman. You can't say things like that and expect me to behave. I'm only human."

Sunny smiled at his discomfort. The feeling was mutual. One glance her way and she wanted to get naked with him. "How far to our destination?"

"We're staying here tonight. I booked us two rooms at a B&B."

"Is it too early to check in?"

CHAPTER FOUR

She would be the death of him. He'd never wanted, needed, a woman as much as he did Sunny Sheldon.

He checked the GPS and the dashboard clock. Too early to check into their room. He'd planned to spend the early part of the afternoon scoping out the town and getting a look at the real estate office where Will and Jessica inquired about the property for sale. Now all he wanted to do was find a secluded place where he could rip Sunny's clothes off and fuck her senseless.

This wasn't like him. He'd always been able to compartmentalize his life. Women and sex in one drawer. Work in another. Family in still another walled-off room. Sunny breached all his walls. This was supposed to be a working trip, but it crossed the family/work line from the beginning. Then he'd added Sunny into the mix and turned his ordered world upside down.

At the moment, he didn't give a flying fuck about Will's case. All he could think about was seeing Sunny's skin in the soft light filtered through the leaves of the surrounding trees, her legs spread for him, her cries of ecstasy echoing on a breeze.

Fuck. He needed to get a grip on reality. The closer they got to town, the less he wanted to get there. Searching the passing landscape, he prayed he'd find what he was looking for. Then it was there, a slight break in the tree line up ahead. No signs. No mailboxes. A logging road, if he had to guess. He slowed, eyeing the well-worn track. Nothing indicated recent use. *Perfect.*

Jake cut the wheel, turning down the lane.

"Where are we going?"

"Some place private." His voice sounded like it had been wrenched from his throat with a rusty coat hanger. Need outweighed everything else in his mind. He hoped she felt the same way.

"Oh. Well." Her head swiveled as she took in the scenery bouncing by. "This looks like it fits the bill."

"Yes, it does." From the condition of the road, he guessed no one had been down it in years. When the road widened enough to pull off to the side, he did. Bending to look out the passenger side window, he spied a foot trail leading off into the dense woods. His hand was on the door latch as he spoke. "Come on. Let's see where that goes."

"You're kidding, right?"

He paused, took a deep breath, and let it out. "Do I look like I'm kidding?" He didn't even try to hide the raw need coursing through his system as his gaze met hers.

"No. You look like a man on a mission."

Maybe it was his libido talking, but she wasn't giving off the *I'm in the woods with a serial killer* vibe. He chalked her amiable attitude up to good fortune and said what was on his mind. "I am. You're my mission. I've tried to be a gentleman. Keep my needs under control. But I'm losing the battle. Honestly? I didn't ask you along on this trip to force you into anything. I'd never do that to a woman. I've wanted you since the first time I laid eyes on you, Sunny. You're all I think about. I know you were teasing earlier—about the size of everything in Texas, but I've never wanted to prove the point more than I do right now. I need you. Right. This. Fucking. Minute." In the courtroom, patience was a virtue. Thank god, this wasn't a courtroom because he was fresh out of patience and restraint. Unless she had other ideas, then he'd find some. Enough to honor her wishes. "I got the impression you wouldn't be averse to checking out your premise yourself. Tell me if I'm wrong and I'll turn this rig around and get back on the road."

"What, exactly, did you have in mind?"

"Fucking. In the woods. Horizontal if we can find a suitable place. If not…"

His dick throbbed, aching to be inside her, to claim her here in this forest like a wild animal. He'd never felt so close to the edge. When her lips parted on a breath, he focused on her mouth, hoping he could hear her response over the blood rushing past his ears on its way south.

"I packed a pashmina."

He shook his head, trying to make sense of her words.

"A shawl," she clarified. "We can put down on the ground."

He was out of the vehicle in seconds, opening the back hatch where they'd stowed their luggage. She met him at the rear of the vehicle.

"Here." She grabbed her bag. "It's right on top, I think."

She rummaged around, pulled a brightly colored item out. Jake closed the liftgate, fingered the lock button then reached for her free hand. "Let's go."

They were barely out of sight of the Jeep when they came upon a small clearing. A few stumps formed a rough circle and decaying logs established a perimeter. The field had probably been used as a staging area for the loggers a decade or more ago. When the workers cleared out, they'd left the area to nature. Several trees had grown up inside the ring. Jake stalked over to a shady spot. He kicked leaves and fallen twigs away until he could inspect the ground beneath. Kneeling carefully so as not to break his engorged dick in half, he bent to remove a couple of rocks then held his hand out. Sunny handed over the fabric thing she'd brought. As he spread it out, it pleased him to see it was bigger than he'd thought and would easily shield Sunny's petite frame from the dirty ground. It wasn't the Victorian bed-and-breakfast where he'd made reservations, but it would have to do. He needed her too much to wait for niceties.

Rising to his feet, he vowed to make it up to her later, with a fancy dinner, candlelight, and soft linens. A mattress fit for a queen.

The city reminded him how far man had come from their cave-dweller days, but out here? He was anything but civilized.

"Take your shorts and panties off," he ordered. "Leave your shirt on."

Her eyes lit with a fire from within then, with a nod, she did as he said. When she stood before him, naked from the waist down, a primal urge hit him so hard, his knees threatened to buckle. He pointed to the pallet. "Lay down. Hands above your head. Legs spread."

Silent, she complied.

He stood over her, looking his fill. *Fuck*, she was beautiful, her surrender complete. Moisture glistened on her folds. She was wet for him, and he hadn't touched her yet. He'd been with his share of women, some he'd tapped more than once, but never, ever, had a woman tempted him the way Sunny did. Tonight, in their soft bed, he'd bring her to the brink with his mouth before he gave in and filled her. But nightfall was hours away. This afternoon, in these woods, he'd take. And take. And take.

His hands shook as he fished a condom out of his wallet and freed his dick from its prison. He stroked himself, once, twice, never taking his eyes off the woman in front of him. She lay still, watching him, her hips rising in invitation as he sheathed himself then dropped to his knees between her legs. He shoved his jeans down his thighs then shimmied closer, lifting her ass into the air, fitting the head of his cock to her entrance.

"I've changed my mind. I want to see your tits."

She nodded, giving him permission. Slowly, he unbuttoned her blouse, pushing it open to reveal a plain bra that was sexier in its innocence than any lace gizmo he'd ever seen. He closed his hands over the twin cotton-clad mounds, squeezing. His dick jerked, begging him to get on with it. Instead, he sat back on his heels, taking in the view.

Sunny Sheldon in a state of dishabille, in the woods, on the brink of being fucked by a caveman, was radiant. Her skin glowed with life, and desire lit her eyes. Her nipples were hard pebbles beneath their modest covering. The scent of her arousal wafted on the warm breeze, taunting him to take what was his. What she freely gave to him.

He wanted it more than he wanted his next breath. He wanted her. Not for today. Not for this trip. Forever.

For. Fucking. Ever.

The thought barreled through him like a freight train out of control. He couldn't stop it. Didn't want to stop it.

Rising to his knees again, he fingered her sex, lined his cock up with her entrance, then, arms wrapped around her thighs to hold her in place, he drove into her hard. His balls slapped against her ass.

Mine.

Again.

Mine.

Again.

Mine.

He was close to coming. A scrap of civility broke through his caveman thoughts. She would come before he did. Always.

He fingered her clit. Her eyes flew open, burning him with her gaze. Then her hand was on his wrist, her hips moving with him, taking him impossibly deeper into her core. He stroked her nub until the first fluttering of her internal muscles hinted of her impending release.

Her body tensed then, on a cry loud enough to startle birds from the trees, she fell apart for him.

Jake released his hold on her thighs and pinned her beneath him. He drove into her repeatedly. Claiming her orgasm as his. Taking, taking, taking. Until her sweet, responsive body wrenched control. Taking. Taking. Taking.

❧❧

Her body hummed with satisfaction. Jake's weight atop her felt like a security blanket protecting her from the world.

She recalled the moment she'd realized he was serious about doing it in the woods. The closest she'd ever come to outdoor sex was doing it with the window open. She'd worried the whole time someone would hear her and Ian. She'd experienced similar worries today. What if someone came along? What if they were in someone's backyard and didn't even know it? Jake ordered her to take her shorts and panties off, and as she'd stood before him naked from the waist down, exposed and vulnerable, her worries evaporated under his heated gaze.

A thought popped into her head, and she chuckled.

Jake nuzzled her neck. "What's so funny?"

"You never got to see my tits."

He growled and nipped at the skin below her ear. "Damned sexiest bra I've ever seen—bar none."

"I thought men preferred lace."

"Lace is good. Cotton is better." Pushing to one elbow, he cupped her breast with his free hand. "You weren't trying to seduce me, and that's what did it for me. You were just being you."

"You should have seen the panties I wore. They weren't sexy, either."

"Wear them for me later?" He pushed one cup up to expose her breast. Her nipple tightened as the soft air wafted across it. "Damn, you're going to be the death of me."

His cock twitched inside her, growing hard again. He flexed his hips, drawing a pained groan from his lips. "What are the chances this condom has one more round in it? 'Cause if it doesn't, I'll have to dig one out of my luggage."

"I'm on the pill."

"I'm clean. My right hand is the only partner I've been

with for god knows how long.
You sure it's okay, baby?"

Needing to touch him, she grabbed his ass with both hands. "I'm sure. You can take it off if you want."

As he stared into her eyes, his cock swelled inside her. "Next time." He kissed the tip of her nose. "I'm so hard I'd probably come if I tried to get the damn thing off."

"Next time, then." She dug her nails into his taut cheeks, urging him to go deeper.

He took the hint, moving slowly in and out of her sensitive channel like time didn't matter. She supposed it didn't, unless a hiker or homeowner or some form of wildlife ran across them. As he bent and took her nipple into his mouth, every thought but one flew out of her head. She needed more of his skin against hers.

Running her hands up under his T-shirt, she shoved the fabric up around his shoulders. He took the hint, releasing her breast long enough to grab the back of his shirt and yank it over his head. He pulled his arms free then the garment sent up a plume of dust as it landed behind her head. She couldn't have cared less as he pushed the other side of her bra up and resumed his task of driving her crazy.

Cradling his head in one hand, she urged him on while her other hand explored every inch of taut skin within reach. There seemed to be miles of it stretched over firm muscles that shifted and rippled as he moved above and inside her. She loved his strength, held in check as he took her gently, but she'd loved it even more when need overruled civility. The two sides of Jake Ingram. The civilized attorney, negotiating a satisfactory outcome for both parties, and the Philistine, taking what he wanted with little concern for niceties. Both intrigued her beyond reason.

CHAPTER FIVE

What the hell was he doing?

Jake reached down, gathered up the shawl thingy Sunny had provided, enabling his moment of insanity. With his back to her, he folded the colorful swath of fabric while she dressed. She'd been 100 percent complicit in what they'd done, but since his blood supply was feeding more than one piece of his anatomy, he recognized how impulsive and selfish he'd been.

This wasn't him. He lived a measured, regimented, planned-to-the-maximum life. He controlled his needs. Never let them overrule his common sense or his ingrained sense of decency. But he'd done so today. He'd let his desire for Sunny off the leash. Let it run rampant.

Shit. He owed her an apology. He gave up trying to fold the fabric into a neat bundle and turned, prepared to beg her forgiveness and promise anything for a chance to make it up to her. Her timid smile made his knees weak and his heart stammer. Standing in this wild place with her mussed hair and skin flushed from a recent orgasm, she looked like a goddess. Despite his remorse for taking her in such a primitive way, he had the urge to beat his chest and shout like a crazed caveman. He'd done that to her. And god, he wanted to do it again. And again. And again. Ad infinitum.

He held out the ball of fabric. "I'm sorry."

She took the offering and shook it, dislodging a shower of grass and twigs. "It's washable. Don't worry about it."

It took a second for his brain to catch up. When it did, he laughed. "I wasn't apologizing for ruining your…what did you call it?"

"Pashmina."

He nodded, not even trying to push the unfamiliar word past his lips. "I meant, I'm sorry for losing control. For taking you here." He swept his hand out to indicate the clearing. "You deserve better."

"I don't know, Jake. If it got any better, I might not survive it. But I sure hope we can try."

The spark of humor in her eyes and the slight quirk of her lips hit him at the same time his brain registered what she'd said. "You aren't mad?"

"Why would I be? If I'd said no, we would have stopped, wouldn't we?" She didn't give him time to answer. "I wanted this as much as you. Back in the truck, you said you wanted me from the first minute you saw me. I wanted you just as much. After you went home, I hoped you would call me or come back. I can't tell you how many nights I lay in bed, wishing I'd had just one night with you before you left. I understand why you kept your distance then. You needed to make sure I had nothing to do with stealing your brother's paintings. I'm glad that's been cleared up because I can tell you, once will not be enough, Jake."

He closed the distance between them, took her in his arms. She lifted her face, and he bent to crush his lips to hers. A moan escaped as her lips parted, allowing him entrance. He tasted her, letting his lips and tongue promise all manner of wicked things he intended to do to her. Breaking away while he still had the presence of mind to do so, he met her gaze. "I still maintain you deserve better than a tumble in the woods, and you sure as hell deserve better than me."

"You could be right," she countered. "I'll need more data to come to a firm conclusion."

He rocked against her, showing her what she did to him. "Tell me one thing."

"What?" She stroked his nape.

"Do you have enough data to support the saying everything is bigger in Texas?"

Her face flushed a becoming shade of pink. She reached between them, cupped his growing erection. "God, yes. You've got a cannon, Jake. Impressive." She tightened her grip on him. "You've ruined me for other men."

At the mention of other men, Jake's caveman instincts reared to life again. Digging his fingers into her ass cheeks, he lifted her, brought her flush against him. In a move he recognized as macho bullshit but was unable to curb, he took her mouth with his—kissing the evil words from her lips. The same mantra he'd heard as he'd claimed her on the hard-packed ground came back to him, echoing in the recesses of his brain. *Mine. Mine. Mine.*

She shimmied in his arms, bringing him to his senses. He let her go, expecting her to put as much distance between them as possible. Instead, she pushed her shorts and panties to her ankles, and as she stepped out of them, reached for the button on his jeans. "Hurry, Jake. I need you. Now."

He didn't need to be told twice. He brushed her hands away then made short work of the fastenings. As soon as he'd pushed his jeans and boxers past his hips, she wrapped her arms around his neck. She hopped. He caught her in his arms, lifted her so the tip of his cock notched into her wet, heated entrance.

Resting her elbows on his shoulders, she fisted her hands in his hair, dragging his head back. "Fuck me, Jake. Hard. Fast. Now."

This time it was her lips crushing his as he lowered her onto his aching shaft. She felt so damned good, he was in danger of passing out from the sheer pleasure of being inside her. He fought to stay in the moment, unwilling to miss a second of the best sex he'd ever experienced. And recent drought aside, he'd been with more than his share of women, and he'd never taken one without a barrier between them. Never wanted to until now. As he helped her move on him, something shifted inside him. A key piece of who he was, who he wanted to be, tumbled, and fell into place.

❧

She could ride him like this forever, she mused as she took what she wanted. Him. Inside her. Stretching her. Filling her. Skin-to-skin for the first time. As much as she loved his Texas-sized cock, she wanted to experience the rush of his hot cum shooting against her womb when he lost control. Nothing would come of it, but she wanted to be his. Wanted him to mark her. Claim her in a way no one else ever had.

It was very cave woman of her, but he brought something primal out in her. Or maybe it was this place, this magical place they'd stumbled upon. There'd be time to test her theory later—if they survived. The way her heart raced, she wasn't sure she'd make it, but if death was the price for these few minutes of bliss, she'd pay up and die with a smile on her face.

Was it possible he was even harder this time than he'd been before? She wrenched her lips away from his, raised her face to the sun, and bowed her back, supporting herself by digging her fingers into his shoulders. He buried his face between her breasts, his teeth working at the buttons of her blouse. His hot breath through the layers of shirt and bra nearly sent her over the edge as she silently vowed the next time, they'd be naked. Completely naked.

"Feels so good," she ground out as he moved inside her. "Don't stop."

Jake growled into the cleavage he'd exposed. Then his lips latched on to the top of her left breast, and he sucked at the tender skin. Marking her. There wasn't anything gentle about his assault, and she wouldn't have it any other way. The bite of pain tripped every nerve ending, sent an electric jolt to the spot where their bodies became one. She dropped her head to his shoulder, biting down on the corded muscles as she came in a rush of pain and pleasure so intense, she teetered on the edge of consciousness. Jake thrust into her until he, too, couldn't hold out any longer. He threw his head back and roared his pleasure for the world to hear.

Arms wrapped tight around his neck, Sunny collapsed against his chest. They stood there, connected in the most intimate way possible, clinging to each other as their breathing slowly evened out. Sunny'd never been more content. Jake's cock remained impressively hard even as the evidence of their mingled pleasure trickled from her channel. A smile broke across her face as she raised her head enough to flick his earlobe with the tip of her tongue. Then she whispered in his ear. "We made a mess, Counselor."

His laughter vibrated through her body then his hands squeezed her bare ass cheeks. "Give me a minute. I'm having a little trouble remembering which planet we're on."

Sunny found the energy to raise up. Their gazes met. "Does that happen often?"

"Never. You sent me into orbit, woman." He leaned in for a kiss, and she met him halfway. His lips were hot and firm, and she wanted to feel them on another part of her body. Jake Ingram knew how to make a woman feel like a goddess.

They parted when, by silent mutual agreement, they came up for air. Sunny's legs trembled, and she wasn't sure she'd be able to stand, but they couldn't remain where they were indefinitely. "We should go," she said.

"My knees are shaking," he admitted.

"Better put me down before you fall."

"No danger of me falling, but I don't want to drop you." He lifted her, and his cock slid free.

Sunny fought the urge to cling to him like a barnacle and beg him to never let her go. With a sigh, she unlocked her legs and he lowered her until her feet met the ground. She wobbled slightly, but Jake was there, holding her close until she pushed away and stood on her own. He righted his clothes then gathered hers from where they'd fallen, shook them free of dirt. She refused the panties, so he knelt in front of her, offering his assistance. Hand on his shoulder, she put one foot into her shorts.

"Hold on to me. I can't leave you like this."

Before she knew what was happening, he lifted her left leg and buried his face between her thighs. Sunny dug her fingers into his scalp and held on for dear life as his tongue swept between her folds. It wasn't her first go-round at oral sex, but in the past, it had been an appetizer before the main course. Jake lapped up their mingled juices like he couldn't get enough. And, lord, she was grateful for his thoroughness. Soon, she directed his movements. Rocking her hips to make all the right parts meet up. He brought her to the brink of a total meltdown then he abruptly changed things up. His lips latched on to her clit and sucked while he drove two fingers into her dripping channel where they instantaneously found some magical button previously unknown to her.

The orgasm took her by surprise. The clench of muscles sharp and painful yet, oddly, cathartic. Her cries of pleasure echoed off the trees ringing the clearing as her body convulsed, purging itself of tension and anxiety. Her leg gave out on her, and Jake was there to scoop her into his arms. She snuggled against his big, powerful chest as he carried her to the Jeep. He propped her against the passenger side and knelt to help her into her shorts. Then he lifted her onto the seat, fastened the seat belt, and closed the door. She was asleep before they made it back to the road.

CHAPTER SIX

Jake drove with one hand on the wheel. Elbow propped on the door, he ran his free hand over his face, reliving every glorious second he'd spent between her legs. He'd gone down on women before, lots of times, but never standing up. He'd intended to help her into her shorts, but their co-mingled scent caught his attention. Then he'd glanced up and saw a trickle of wetness running down her inner thigh—and the urge to taste her, to taste *them*, took over. The next thing he knew, he'd buried his face between her legs. Not only tasting. Eating. Like a goddamn caveman.

She'd tasted so damn good. He couldn't stop. Not until he'd made her come one more time.

He glanced at her slumped against the passenger side door, asleep. Or passed out? He'd behaved like a savage today. Her shirt gaped open where he'd gnawed a button off to get to her skin. The gap revealed the dark bruise rising where he'd marked her.

Christ. He'd done everything but drag her around by the hair while beating his chest to warn all the other cavemen to stay the fuck away from his woman.

He shifted his focus where it belonged—on the road—and reminded himself she wasn't his woman. And as soon as she woke, she'd probably kick his ass to drive the message home. He wouldn't blame her. He deserved her wrath. They hardly knew one another. Yeah, there'd been an attraction right from the start, but he was a grown-ass man. He could control his urges. Except where she was concerned. It had been bad enough before he came back to New York, when he'd jacked off countless times with nothing but his imagination to go on. Now that he'd been inside her—tasted her, tasted them—he didn't know how he'd ever keep his hands off her or his dick out of her.

"Won't be a problem," he mumbled to himself. He might as well turn the Jeep around and take her home. No way was she going to want to spend the next week or two with him.

At a faint moan from the other seat, he put both hands on the wheel and risked another glance at her. Eyes closed, her swollen lips slightly parted in sleep, her skin flushed, and her hair mussed, she looked thoroughly fucked. He chided himself for the lightning bolt of pride stiffening his dick. If she gave any indication she wanted to do it again, he'd pull over and fuck her brains out on the side of the road.

"Get a grip, Ingram." He tore his gaze to the road. The bed-and-breakfast he'd booked was up the road a ways. They were both tired. Maybe he could convince her to spend the night if he promised to take her home first thing in the morning. "Fat chance," he mumbled.

Beside him, she stirred. He caught a glimpse of her arm as she stretched just as they passed a sign for their accommodations. He stopped at the end of the long driveway. "We're here."

She blinked and sat up, taking in their surroundings. The instant she spied the house, her eyes grew round, and she bounced in her seat. "Oh. My. God. Have you ever seen anything like it?"

A three-story Victorian stood in the distance—a relic of another time when big families were the norm and porches connected communities. He'd seen a few in Texas but none as whimsical as this. "It's…interesting."

"It's like something out of a storybook." She pulled the visor down. When she slid the cover off the built-in mirror, a light came on. One glance at her reflection and she turned to him—a big smile on her face. "I look like I've been ravaged by a big, strapping Texan."

Jake sighed. "I'm sorry, Sunny." He glanced at the pastel house at the end of the lane, imagining a hot meal and a comfortable bed. Maybe a shower, though he wasn't in any hurry to wash her scent off his body. "If you want, we can find a drive-thru for dinner then I can drive you home."

"What?" Her expression shifted from confusion to anger in the blink of an eye. "Are you trying to get rid of me? Did I do something wrong? Oh wait. I jumped you. Is that it? You don't like women who know what they want and go for it? Well, let me set you straight, Mr. Macho Man. This is the twenty-first century and women have needs, too!" With a huff, she sat back and, staring straight ahead, crossed her arms over her midsection. The move made her blouse gape even more.

Jake fixated on the bruise he'd put on her. There was something about the mark. It wasn't all enormous, but to anyone with half a brain, it sent a message. Walk away. This one is taken.

Not for the first time, his shoulder ached. He reached up to rub the spot where she'd nearly taken a chunk out of his hide. She'd been the one to initiate their vertical encounter, and he'd been either an ass or a gentleman to take her up on the offer. If he were to believe her words, she was mad because he'd offered to take her home, not because he'd gone caveman on her. A glimmer of hope crept in, lifting his spirits. Time to test the waters.

"You can jump me anytime you want." He shifted the transmission into Park and took his hands off the wheel. "Right now is good."

He was a beast where she was concerned. He'd been hard since he'd inhaled their mingled scent. It was a wonder he'd managed to drive, with his groin commanding most of his blood supply.

She turned a haughty glare on him then her gaze dropped to his lap and the obvious bulge behind his zipper. "We can't do it here. We're blocking their driveway."

She had to be kidding, but the expression on her face said otherwise. He chuckled. "No, I don't suppose right this minute would be appropriate. How about we check in, get cleaned up and find some dinner. If you're going to jump me again, I'm going to need some sustenance."

The wicked intent in her smile made his dick twitch. "What are you waiting for? Let's get this show on the road."

"Yes, ma'am." Jake shifted in his seat and put the car back in Drive.

❧

Jake insisted they keep both rooms he'd reserved despite Sunny's protests. No one this far from the city knew who she was, and she didn't care who found out she and the Texan were sleeping together, though there'd yet to be any actual sleep.

Still wearing the clothes she'd arrived in, she sprawled across the comfy bed in her room, arms stretched over her head, reliving every moment they'd spent in the woods. If she closed her eyes, she could smell the pine and hear the birds in the trees. She smiled, recalling the way Jake apologized for having sex in such a primitive place. Always the gentleman, except when it came to shagging her. Then his enthusiasm overrode his manners in a way she genuinely appreciated. He didn't seem to believe her when she said she wasn't the least bit offended by their impromptu sexathon. She'd have to work on convincing him because the sex today was by far the best ever.

A glance at the clock on the bedside table reminded her she needed to get a move on. The proprietor of the B&B recommended a restaurant a few miles down the road. She and Jake parted ways, agreeing to meet in the lobby in an hour, which meant she needed to hustle, or she'd be late.

Both of their rooms boasted private bathrooms, a luxury she appreciated as she eyed the ancient claw-foot tub and its equally antiquated shower system. It all looked to be in working order, but it didn't lend itself to a shared experience. If Jake's room boasted a similar setup, his head would probably stick out above the curved shower curtain rod, and he'd have to stand sideways in the tub to keep his broad shoulders from touching the wraparound curtain. She chuckled to herself, imagining the scene.

As she adjusted the temperature, she took in the depth and width of the old slipper-style tub and decided it could easily seat two in tandem. She pulled the curtain closed, flipped the valve to send the water up to the showerhead, then stepped into the tub. A quick rinse would do for now, and, with a little luck, she could talk Jake into a nice, long bath after dinner, followed by some very uncivilized sex on an actual mattress.

With her new goal in mind, she hurried through her routine and dressed in clean capri pants and a lightweight blouse; she arrived in the lobby one minute early to find Jake waiting for her. He'd changed into dark jeans and a dress shirt in a lighter shade of blue that matched his eyes. As a nod to the heat, he'd left the top two buttons undone and rolled the sleeves up to expose his muscular forearms. "I see you figured out the shower."

His gaze raked her from head to toe. An appreciative smile broke across his face. "It wasn't easy, but I can tell you, I have something in mind for that tub later."

Perhaps it wouldn't be hard to talk him into a bath after all. "I had a similar thought. Maybe we could discuss your plans and mine over a thick steak and a baked potato? Perhaps we can merge our visions into one?"

"Mergers are my specialty," he said as he reached for her hand and steered her toward the door.

Suddenly, she wanted to get the dinner portion of the evening over with as soon as possible. She'd yet to see all of

Jake Ingram at one time, and her imagination was working overtime to fill the gap. Their activities earlier in the day provided a lot of data to inform her fantasies, but being able to explore every inch of his wet, slippery body was high on her list of priorities. On the front porch, she waited until he'd shut the door then she tugged him down the steps and across the yard to where they'd parked the Jeep.

"In a hurry?" he asked as he climbed into the driver's seat and pressed the ignition button.

"I'm not going to lie, Counselor. I see a merger in my future and I'm a tad bit impatient to get started."

"Are you, now?"

She almost swooned at the way he'd exaggerated his Southern drawl. God, could he be sexier? "And you aren't?"

"Didn't say that, sweetheart. Just didn't want to assume a merger was a given tonight. After what we did earlier…"

She sighed. He'd done the perfect gentleman thing again. "I'm fine, Jake. Except for the ache in a certain location I can't reach. I need your help, if you get my meaning?"

He braked at an intersection, waited his turn to proceed, then pressed the accelerator. Only then did he glance her way. "You sure it's only an ache? You aren't sore?"

"Not sore. But I will be sorely pissed if you don't do something about this aching as soon as we get back to the B&B."

His lips quirked up on one side. "I think I've got another merger in me." He glanced down at his lap, drawing her gaze there. He would cause a stir if he walked into the restaurant with a huge bulge leading the way.

Sunny licked her lips. She'd given a few blow jobs in the past, but they'd always been for the guy's benefit, not hers. Biting her bottom lip, she examined the thought running through her brain. Jake would enjoy the gesture but so would she. He'd tasted her earlier. It was her turn, wasn't it?

He pulled into the parking area. It was a large lot, testament to the popularity of the restaurant, but tonight there were only a handful of cars all occupying the front row of marked slots. Jake steered the Jeep toward an open one. Before he could shift into Park, Sunny covered his hand with hers.

"Maybe we could park over there?" She pointed to a row of empty slots on the fringe of the main lot. By day, the towering trees nearby probably provided great shade. This late in the evening, they cast a deep shadow. Not a suitable place if you were scared of the dark, but perfect if you wanted a bit of privacy.

Jake eyed the remote area then his gaze met hers. "I'm not fucking you in a parking lot."

"I have something else in mind." She moved her hand to cup his impressive erection. "You can't walk in like that."

His eyes searched hers for a long, silent moment. "I planned to let you go in first. Give myself a few minutes to get it under control."

"Let me help. Please?" To sweeten the offer, she licked her lips in what she hoped was a salacious manner. She'd never needed to convince a man to let her suck his dick. They were usually whipping it out, begging. Just another way Jake differed from the jerks she'd dated in the past.

"You're sure? I can master it myself. You know, think of puppies in a kennel or my fifth-grade math teacher."

"Not necessary. I want to do this. Please?"

He scrubbed both hands over his face then returned them to the steering wheel. He took his foot off the brake. "I must be losing my mind."

Once he'd parked, scooted his seat as far from the steering wheel as possible and reclined the seatback, she considered the logistics. The stationary console would be an obstacle, but one she'd manage.

"I'd recline more, but I want to watch. Do you mind?"

"Not if you don't mind me doing the best I can. I knew you were big, but…"

"You'll do fine, sweetheart. Just open your mouth and I'll do the rest."

She wrapped her fingers around the base, took over the

slow stroke he'd been doing for himself. "You're beautiful, Jake. If I could, I'd paint you, just like this." She placed her free hand on his belly, slid it upward, taking his shirttails with it. "I can't wait to get you naked so I can see all of you."

"Which reminds me. I still haven't seen your tits. Mind if I touch while you, you know?"

"Not at all. Be my guest." She bent over the console and flicked her tongue out, taking her first taste of Jake Ingram at the same time his giant hand clamped down on her breast. His rough touch triggered a gush of liquid heat between her legs. If he kept it up, she'd have her own embarrassment to contend with when they entered the restaurant. But that was a worry for another time. Jake Ingram was right where she wanted him. Opening her mouth wide, she took him as deep as she could then lifted her head, letting his length slide through her lips.

"Fuuuuck."

Jake's hips rose then settled back against the seat as she dove again, taking him even deeper the second time. This time when she pulled up, she applied pressure to his stomach, urging him to stay still. He abandoned her breast, using both hands to grip the headrest as she repeated the process. This time, she took almost all of him, which brought her nose close enough to inhale his intoxicating male scent. If they were anywhere but a parking lot, she'd take the time to nuzzle him right there, lick his balls, familiarize herself with every inch of him. But if his profanity-laced commentary was any sign, he wouldn't last long.

The thought filled her with pride. She didn't think for a minute her technique was perfect, but she congratulated herself on making Jake want her so much. She did this to him. Reduced him to swear words and made him throw out the rule book to have sex in the woods and chance a blow job in a parking lot. He made her just as crazy. One word from him and she'd shimmy out of her pants and climb on top of him, right here. Right now.

The ache between her legs was becoming more insistent

with every sloppy repetition. She'd drooled all over his shaft, her hand, and even his boxers tucked beneath his balls were growing damp. This was messy and amateurish, but Jake didn't seem to mind.

In the woods, he'd held so much power over her, but here, he was at her mercy. It was a heady thought, and she took full advantage, pulling off him to stroke him slowly with her hand. The move wrenched a frustrated groan from him, followed by a plea for her to put him out of his misery.

"I won't last, baby. Thirty seconds, tops. My balls are halfway up my throat, ready to detonate. Please, baby."

She knew exactly how he felt. She was about two seconds from exploding as well. "Put your hand down my pants. Touch me," she said, shifting a little more to allow him access.

When he slid his hand in, found her wet folds, she closed her eyes, savored his touch for a couple heartbeats before returning her focus to his pleasure. A pearly bead of pre-cum formed on the tip of his cock. A swipe of her tongue took care of it before she took him deep again. His taste lingered in her mouth, and for the first time ever, she wanted to swallow every drop. But this was Jake, and he wasn't asking her to do anything. This entire crazy episode had been her idea, and she wanted to see it through to the very end, hoping it would be a satisfying one for him.

His fingers felt so good on her. Stroking, plunging inside her channel, teasing her to the brink then retreating. His other hand maintained a tight grip on the headrest as he tried to control his body's instinct to thrust. He was slowly losing the battle, his movements becoming more pronounced with each bob of her head until he surrendered. Moving his hand to grip her head, he held her down while he rocked into her, the swollen head of his cock hitting the back of her throat repeatedly until he lost the battle. He came with a shout she feared would bring people running from the restaurant to see what was going on. Sunny held on to his cock with one hand and his shirt with the other, determined to ride it out, to take everything he gave.

When he'd spent his load, his entire body relaxed, except for the hand down her pants. She released his cock, and he guided her head to his lap. "Let me make you come," he said. "You're close."

Sunny shifted enough to enable her to slide her hand alongside his. She gripped his wrist and hung on as he worked her up fast and hard. In a matter of minutes, she buried her face in his lap and screamed as her body reached its limit and she tumbled headlong into pleasure.

She didn't know how long they lay there, both wrung out and satisfied, before another type of hunger took over and propelled them to straighten their clothes. Jake raised his seatback and powered the seat to its original position while Sunny did the best she could to clean herself with a tissue from her purse. She didn't dare look at her hair. It had to be a mess. "Do we have to go in there? A drive-thru sounds mighty good right now."

"You're looking mighty good," Jake said as he started the engine and put the Jeep in gear. "The just-fucked look suits you."

"You're looking relaxed yourself, cowboy. Did you have an enjoyable ride?"

"The best." He checked the back-up camera for obstacles then glanced her way. "You can suck my dick anytime you want. Just give me a little notice if I'm driving so I can pull off the road. I think I went blind there for a few seconds."

"If you're trying to say thank you, then you're welcome. You have some wicked hand skills yourself. Thank you for taking care of my needs."

He nodded acceptance of her words. "I think there's a Mickey D's a little farther down the road. I'd hoped to feed you a little better, but I don't think either of us is up to sitting in a fancy restaurant right now."

"Can we get the food to go? I'm okay with eating in the car."

"Or, we can take it back to my room and eat it naked."
Sunny smiled. "I like your idea better than mine."

CHAPTER SEVEN

They ended up in Sunny's room because it had the larger bed and a small table perfect for two to share a quick meal. Once inside, their stomachs dictated they keep their clothes on long enough to fuel up, but once they'd satisfied one hunger, another took precedent.

"Now for dessert." Jake stood, offered his hand to her. When they stood toe-to-toe, he wrapped his arm around her waist, bringing her even closer. "I'm going to undress you and taste every inch of you as I go. Any objections?"

Sunny shook her head. "Not a one, Counselor, but I reserve the right to do the same to you. Later."

"I don't have a problem with allowing you the same rights. Your conditions will be duly recorded in the transcript."

With Jake nibbling on her neck and working the buttons on her blouse, she found it difficult to think, much less speak. "Oh, I like it when you speak lawyer. It's sexy."

"No one has ever said that to me before." He kissed his way down her chest to the top of her bra. "My profession usually turns women off."

Sunny clasped his head with both hands as he nuzzled her cleavage. Suddenly, he stopped, drew back. He cupped her breast; his thumb brushed a spot above her bra. "What have we here?" he asked before tasting the bruise he'd left on her earlier in the day. "Looks like someone has marked you as his." He kissed the spot again. "Enter this into the record as evidence."

"Evidence of what?" she breathed, holding him tight as he got up close and personal with the mark.

"Evidence that you belong to me."

The possession in his voice made her knees weak and her insides melt. No one had ever claimed her the way Jake Ingram did, and she couldn't find a single reason to object. He yanked her bra cup down, exposing one breast. "Who do you belong to, Sunny?" His tongue laved at her nipple, drawing a moan from her. When he took the hardened bud into his mouth and sucked, she would have crumpled to the floor, but he caught her, tumbled her to the bed, and came down on top of her, held her captive with her arms above her head, their fingers intertwined. "Consider yourself under oath. Tell me the truth, or you'll be held in contempt and punished." His eyes glittered with mischief and a smoldering lust.

"What's your question, Counselor?"

"Who marked you? Who do you belong to?"

He rocked his hips against hers, pressing his hard cock into her belly. She gave a fleeting thought to being on the receiving end of his punishment but decided they could circle back to the discussion when she wasn't desperate to feel him inside her. Sunny tilted her hips and spread her legs wider, inviting him to take what he wanted. "You. I belong to y—"

Jake's mouth came down on hers, swallowing the rest of her declaration with a kiss that cemented his claim on her body and incinerated his vow to go slow. She added going slow to her list of things they could explore later then went to work on the buttons of his shirt. In a blur of motion and acrobatics, her blouse joined his shirt and jeans on the floor, followed by her bra, shorts, and panties.

"These have to go, too." She slipped her hands beneath the waistband of his boxers.

Jake flashed her a smile filled with wicked intent. "No objection whatsoever."

He shimmied out of the confining garment then sat back on his heels, allowing her to look her fill. She'd seen her share of nude men, but Jake put them all to shame. A light dusting of hair across his pecs accented his broad chest. The taut skin across his defined abs she'd briefly touched earlier when she'd tried to keep him from interrupting her exploration of his other endowments. Her gaze traveled south, following an arrow of hair that merged with a thatch of curls at the base of his cock. A rush of possessiveness washed over her at the sight of his erection standing hard and proud. For her.

"I don't manscape." He didn't sound the least bit apologetic for not bowing to what she considered a ridiculous practice. She'd never seen the appeal of the Ken doll look. Jake was all man, and she loved it.

"And I hope you never do." She sat up. "Can I touch?"

"I'm not sure how long I can hold out once you put your hands on me, but go ahead."

❧❧

Jake promised himself he'd take it slow with her this time, but the second she ran her fingers through the light patch of hair on his right pec, his resolve faltered. She was his Kryptonite. Her touch shredded the control he'd always prided himself on. He didn't use women. Didn't take them like a caveman. He'd always been a considerate lover, making sure his partner found her pleasure before he sought his own. One touch from Sunny Sheldon and he was in danger of going off like a Roman candle, and her hand wasn't anywhere near his cock.

When it came to her, he was a different person. Crazy. Out of control. Insatiable. Since his college days, he could count on one hand the women he'd been with more than once. One and done. It had always been enough for him. There were too many available women to get hung up on one. Of the ones he'd gone back to for more, he'd quickly grown tired of and ended it after a few weeks.

Sunny was different. They'd only been hooking up for a day, but he couldn't keep his hands off the woman. All he had to do was look at her and his blood supply rushed to his dick. Seeing the mark he'd put on her earlier in the day, he swallowed hard. He hadn't marked a woman since high school when he'd put a hickey on Jane Hansen's neck. She'd slapped him silly the next day when she'd been obliged to wear a turtleneck to school on one of the hottest days of the year. He'd learned his lesson. Girls, women, didn't appreciate the possessive gesture. Or maybe Jane was the only one. Didn't matter. Her wrath cured him of the need to mark a woman. Until Sunny. To distract himself from what her hands were doing, he reached out, brushed his finger over the purple bruise on her breast. "I'm sorry. I shouldn't have done this to you."

Her hands stilled. "Don't be. I like it." She placed her hand over his, pressing his palm over the spot. "It makes me horny every time I see it."

"You aren't just saying so to please me?"

"Why would I? I like the way you lose control—like you've got to have me."

"I want to do it again." He mentally palm-slapped his forehead even as he pushed her backward, used his superior weight to anchor her to the mattress. He caught her hands in his, stretched them above her head, then buried his face in the crook of her neck. "Right here. For everyone to see."

"Do it. Mark me, Jake. Please."

He couldn't deny her anything, so he drew her delicate skin between his lips and sucked until she writhed beneath him and spread her legs, inviting him in. Flexing his hips, he took her in one, brutal thrust, forcing a gasp from her. When she rocked her hips upward, he sank deeper. Determined to last as long as possible, or at least until she came, he forced himself to remain still. Sunny wiggled beneath him. He released his hold on her neck to look into her eyes. "Don't. I won't last."

Her eyes were dark with lust, her expression desperate. "I'm not going to last, either. I'm hurting, Jake."

"A good hurt?" He'd die if he'd caused her unwanted pain.

"It will be as soon as you start moving."

His gaze dropped to the fresh mark forming on her neck. "I marked you again. This one will be harder to hide."

Her head thrashed on the pillow as she used her hips to force him to get on with it. Her moan was the sexiest thing he'd ever heard. Her gaze met his head-on with a look of determination that made his heart stutter then slam against his chest. "Fuck me, Jake. Hard and fast."

⋘⋙

They were late for breakfast the next morning, but Sunny couldn't have cared less about missing out on the hot meal. Passionate sex won out over food anytime. The fast food they'd consumed the night before fueled multiple sexy sessions but had more than worn off. As they packed their bags and left the cozy accommodations, Sunny's stomach rumbled. "Do we have time to grab some breakfast?" she asked as she handed her bag off to Jake.

He tossed the carry-on sized suitcase into the Jeep, slammed the liftgate shut, and turned to her, took her in his arms. "I wouldn't change a thing about last night or this morning, but I wish we'd booked a place with room service. I'm starving. How about we try the diner we saw on Main Street? It's only about a block from the real estate office. We can walk there after we get some food in us."

"Sounds good to me." After a brief kiss that promised a more heated session later, they parted and climbed into the vehicle. Sunny buckled her seat belt. "I could eat the south end of a northbound horse."

Jake chuckled. "You sound like a Texan."

"Really?" She beamed at him. "I think I might like

Texas."

"You might."

A sign inside the door instructed them to seat themselves, and the smell of bacon and coffee encouraged them to seek out the last empty table against the wall next to the bathrooms. Like all the other tables, the chairs were mismatched. Photographs encompassing everything from high school graduation and wedding pics to birthday celebrations rested beneath thick glass on the tabletop. A condiment rack held laminated menus and a supply of flatware tightly wrapped in paper napkins. As they perused the menus, their server sauntered over, turned the mugs right-side up, and filled them from a steaming carafe.

"What can I get 'cha?" the woman asked, setting the pot on the table so she could extract an order pad and pencil from her apron.

Sunny ordered the Farmer's Breakfast, an enormous platter filled with breakfast meats, eggs, and biscuits. "Can I also get a large orange juice, please?"

"No problem, hon." She turned her attention to Jake. "What about you?"

"I'll have what she's having but with a side of pancakes. Ditto on the orange juice, too."

The waitress retrieved the coffee carafe then departed with a promise to return with their juice glasses.

Sunny's gaze met Jake's. "Do you think we ordered too much food?"

"I didn't see the south end of a northbound horse on the menu, so I improvised." His lips curved up on the ends, and his eyes twinkled. He lifted the white ceramic mug to his lips and took a sip. "I worked up an appetite, too, you know."

"Oh, I know. And, I meant to tell you how much I appreciated the effort you put out last night. And this morning," she added.

"You're welcome. I need to take care of myself today so I can do it again tonight. And tomorrow morning." He winked. "If you want to."

Sunny sighed. "I don't see myself ever turning down a night with you." She sipped her coffee, which smelled a lot better than it tasted. She grabbed two thimble-sized packets of cream and stirred them in before taking another sip. "If I think too much about what we did, I'll end up jumping you right here in the diner. I don't think the other patrons would appreciate the show, so why don't you tell me why we're here?"

They sat back as their server placed two enormous glasses of orange juice on the table. "Food's coming up soon," she said then left them alone again.

Jake picked up the conversation. "We're here because Will and Jessica stopped to inquire about buying a house in the area. I want to find out if Jessica came back later with someone else to look at the property—or another one."

"You think Jessica and Cecil might be nearby?" She couldn't help scanning the other diners to see if anyone looked familiar.

"Relax. Neither one of them has ever met me, and you said you've only met them a few times. I suspect you weren't wearing shorts, and you probably wore your hair up in a fancy do for the occasion."

She mentally willed her shoulders to relax. "You're right. I think the only time I met either of them was at a gallery opening. I usually wear a cocktail dress to those events. Lots of makeup and my hair up."

"What kind of cocktail dress?"

She brought her mug to her lips, looking at him over the rim. "Why do you want to know?"

"I want to picture you in it."

His eyes gave away his wicked thoughts. "Stop. We can't do this here." She glanced around to see if anyone was watching them. "Besides, we need food. Remember?" It was time to change the subject. "What will you do if you find Jessica and Cecil?"

"When. When I find them."

"Okay. When you find them. You aren't going to

confront them yourself, are you?"

"I'm not stupid. I'll enlist the help of the local law enforcement, but I will have a word with them. They have a lot to answer for."

Sunny nodded. "No argument from me. Their duplicity rocked the art world. Especially in New York. Artists are wary about who they trust."

"Has your business suffered because of it?"

She shrugged. "Maybe. A couple of young, new artists did come in, asked a lot of questions, then decided not to consign anything with me."

The server returned with their food then, a short time later, came back to refill their coffee mugs. They abandoned conversation to dive into the plates heaped with delicious-smelling food.

At long last, Jake reopened their last conversation. "What kind of questions did the artists ask?"

She slathered blackberry jam on a biscuit. "They wanted to know if I'd known the people involved. Ours is a small world. I knew if I denied knowing any of the parties involved, the lie would come back to bite me in the ass, so I told the truth." When he didn't reply, she glanced up from her plate. His smile promised many things, none of which were appropriate for where they were. "What?"

"I'd like to bite your ass."

A rush of heat flooded her system. She ducked her head, reached for her juice, and took a long, cooling drink. "You have a one-track mind, Counselor."

"Not true. I can process several things at once. For example, are you sure the people who asked those questions were really artists? Could they have been looking for these two, same as we are?"

She mulled his question over while she chewed a slice of bacon. "You could be right. I didn't know either of the two I recall coming in. And I don't remember hearing about their work going on display in any of the usual places. Which means absolutely nothing. If they ended up consigning at one of the smaller galleries, I probably wouldn't hear about it. It's impossible to keep up with every gallery in the city."

"Makes me wonder though. I've always found it hard to believe Will was their first and only target."

"You think they've been scamming other artists all along?"

"Maybe." He shrugged and sat back to drink his coffee. "The attack on Will's livelihood could be a personal vendetta. A crime of passion—of sorts. No murder involved, thankfully."

"That we know of," Sunny corrected. "After what they pulled, I wouldn't put anything past them. How far would they go to protect their secret? That's why I asked what your intentions were when you find them. I don't want you getting yourself killed."

Jake sat forward, placed his hand over the rim of his juice glass, and turned the container in circles. "Two days ago, I would have said it didn't matter if I died." His gaze speared hers. "Now, I'm thinking I have something to live for."

Sunny was still processing his statement when their server returned with the coffeepot. They both waived her off, so she left the ticket with instructions to pay up front. Jake glanced at his watch. "The office should be open."

He tossed a generous tip on the table then stood and made his way to the register. Sunny followed in a daze. She didn't know which part of Jake's statement she wanted clarified most. The part about it not mattering if he died or the part about having something to live for now. Both made her palms sweat and her heart race. Jake Ingram was an enigma.

CHAPTER EIGHT

Jake silently cursed himself for saying the things he'd
said. He'd broken the lawyer code and his own personal
code—the one about keeping your damn mouth shut. What
was it about Sunny Sheldon that made him act like a caveman
one minute and a lovesick idiot the next? He should tell her
to cover up the hickey he'd given her last night. The damn
thing was distracting. It was a visual reminder of how she felt
under him, her body taking him in, moving with him, coming
apart around him. It was a wonder he could function at all
under the circumstances.

As he handed over his credit card to pay the breakfast
tab, he inhaled deep then let the breath out slow, hoping the
oxygen, followed by a lung cleanse, would help him get his
head on straight. He'd revealed too much about his state of
mind before he came to New York and how this trip changed
his outlook on life. Hustling out to the sidewalk, he didn't
give Sunny an opportunity to question his statements. Her
falling into a quiet step beside him told him she was thinking
up ways to ask what he'd meant.

He'd have to distract her. Their teasing banter over a
jam-covered biscuit came to mind. Yeah, he'd bite her ass
tonight. Leave his mark there, too. Maybe he'd spank her. See
how she liked a little punishment. She'd seemed to like it last

night when he held her hands above her head and took her.

Jake stopped at the corner. He had a goddamn hard-on—again. He couldn't go in the real estate office looking like this. He glanced around at the shop windows for anything to help him focus. His gaze landed on a drugstore display of geriatric supplies. Someone had tied a giant ribbon across an elevated toilet seat. It was both absurd and sobering. Who would think that an appropriate gift, even if the recipient needed it? *Christ. Give the poor person a card or some flowers. Something cheerful. Not a toilet seat!* Though his brother Rick did have a milestone birthday coming up. He'd be thirty in a few weeks and acted like an old man sometimes. Maybe he'd get him one of those. See if it cheered him up or shook him out of whatever doldrums had a hold on him.

By the time the light changed, Jake's erection was well on the way to deflating. He crossed the street, Sunny on his heels. The Open sign hung in the window of the real estate office. He held the door, let Sunny precede him inside.

An older woman with frizzy, graying black hair sat behind a scarred wooden desk. She looked up from her computer monitor, a smile on her bright-red lips. "Good morning! Name's Ruth Winslow. What can I do for you?"

Jake placed his hand on the small of Sunny's back, directed her to one of the visitor chairs facing the desk. He shook hands with Ruth, taking a seat. "I'm Jake and this is Sunny. We were hoping you could help us. My brother and his fiancée stopped in here about six months ago, looking for a place to buy. Maybe you remember them?"

Sunny handed over the photos she'd stashed in her purse. "Do they look familiar?"

Ms. Winslow studied the pictures for a minute. "They asked about a farm listing. Sometimes when I have a lot of inventory, I print the listings out and tape them in the window, hoping someone passing by might see something they like, even if they aren't interested in buying. I can't tell you how many properties I've sold because of those postings." She returned the photos. "I saw them looking.

Waved them in." She shifted a few things around on her already neat desk. "What's this about?"

Jake ignored her question. "Did you show them a property?"

"No. They said they were passing through and weren't ready to buy yet." She stiffened her spine. "I repeat. What is this about?"

"My brother was a victim of a crime perpetrated by his fiancée and another man. The two of them have gone missing. We're trying to locate them." Jake paused, deciding how to phrase his story. "They took everything my brother owned. I promised him I'd find them and get his stuff back."

"What kind of things did they take?"

Sunny jumped into the conversation. "They cleaned out his bank accounts and stole several paintings. Jake's brother is a well-known painter. The canvases are worth a small fortune."

"I see, but isn't this a matter for the police?"

"It is," Sunny agreed. "They're looking into it, but it's a nonviolent crime and the leads have gone cold. We're trying to help."

Jake added, "By any chance, did his fiancée come back later on to look at the property, or another one?"

The woman shook her head. "Not that I know of. I'm the only agent in town. I handle most every listing in this area."

"Did the farm they looked at sell?"

Ruth nodded. "It did. I believe it sold to a couple from the city. An agent out of the next county brought the buyer in. I never saw them myself, but they paid cash and planned to turn it into a free-range chicken farm. Craziest thing I've ever heard of." She huffed out a laugh. "The things these city people think up. I guarantee the place will be on the market within the year. Is your brother still looking to move to the country?"

He smiled at her attempt to sell the not-yet-for-sale property to Will. "No, ma'am. He went home to Texas."

Sunny sat on the edge of her seat. "Can you bring up the listing? I'd like to see the place." She glanced at Jake. He raised an eyebrow at her. "What? I've been thinking of moving someplace quiet. Maybe if I like the looks of it, Ruth can call me when it comes on the market again."

Ms. Winslow typed for a bit before swinging the computer monitor around to show them the pictures of the farm in question. "The house is in great shape for being over a hundred years old. Your brother was most interested in the barn though." She tapped a key, and a montage of photos filled the screen. "It's nearly as ancient as the house, but someone converted the hayloft into an apartment. Lots of light, which makes sense now that I know he's a painter. The barn apartment would be a nice studio."

Jake silently noted the address on the listing. The place would have been perfect for Will, except for being in New York. He hated what happened to Will, vowed he'd make it right, but he wasn't sad the incident brought his brother home.

Sunny asked a few more questions then left the woman her card. "Call me if the property comes back on the market. I'd like to see it."

Hopeful for a future sale, Ruth Winslow escorted them to the door with a smile on her face, not once realizing they'd played her.

"You're going out there, aren't you?"

"Yep. You don't have to go. You can wait at the diner, or I'll drop you at the library or something. They don't know me. I'll pretend I'm lost, ask for directions. See if it's them. If not, no harm done. If it is Cecil and Jessica, I'll come back and visit the local law enforcement, whoever they are. Does a town this size have a police force?"

"Probably not. Most of these small communities rely on the county sheriff's office."

"Perfect for a couple of fugitives."

"I'm going with you. You might not recognize them. All you've ever seen are promotional photos of them from their websites."

"Your choice, but don't get out of the car. They might recognize you."

❦

"Plug the address into the navigation system." Jake rattled off the one he'd memorized from the real estate listing. Sunny tapped the keys on the virtual keyboard.

While the device searched for a route, Sunny rummaged in her purse, came up with a tube of lip balm. She pulled the sun visor down, flipped the cover open to reveal a mirror. As she swiped the soothing goo on her lips, she mumbled, "I hope it's not too far."

The GPS's recorded voice chimed in, "In 300 yards, turn right on Maple Street."

Jake put the Jeep in gear and backed out of the parking space. "If the GPS is correct, it's less than five miles. We'll know if it's them soon."

Sunny was torn. If it was Jessica and Cecil, Jake's business in New York would be done. She had no illusions about him staying there with her. He'd go home when he located the people who'd stolen from his brother or, at the very least, found the paintings. He'd mentioned another lead to follow if this one didn't pan out. "If it's not them, where do we go from here?"

"Callicoon. Cecil Hawthorne's former PR person, a guy by the name of Ross McClelland lives out there. MacKenzie Carlysle took over for him when he retired a few years ago. He worked for Hawthorne a long time. If anyone knows where the man might have gone to hide, McClelland is the man."

"And if he doesn't have information? What will you do then?"

"I don't know. Go home, I guess, and wait for something else to come up. I'm certain they have the paintings and plan to use them, even if it's selling them back to Will, one at a time, to keep them in funds."

"Can he afford to pay them?"

"Depends on what kind of money they want, but, last time I talked to my brother, he said if he saw the paintings again, he'd destroy them himself."

Sunny gasped. "What? Why would he do such a thing?"

"Says they no longer represent him as a painter. He talked about how Jessica convinced him to paint more commercial subjects—things she could sell easily. I guess he went along for a while, and those are the paintings she stole."

"I haven't seen his latest work, but the ones I sold for him were beautiful and appealed to a wide audience. He has a rare talent."

As instructed by the navigation system, Jake made another turn onto a narrow, two-lane road flanked by tall trees on both sides. Mailboxes on posts showed homes existed, but none were visible from the road. "I agree with you. Will is talented. I think he lost his way or, more likely, let Jessica lead him off his path. This entire thing has hit him hard, but he's finding his way out and will be a better person for what he's gone through. Maybe even a better painter, if possible."

"It's possible if he's more in tune with the creative force within himself. If I had any criticism of his early work, it was it lacked a measure of depth. That being said, he has an eye for esthetics few artists possess. I'm sure he's matured as an artist. I hope I get a chance to see what he's working on now. I bet it's spectacular."

"You've got a lot of confidence in a man you hardly know." He slowed the Jeep to take a better look at the number on a mailbox. "This is it." He checked the rearview mirror then stopped in the road as the GPS announced they'd reached their destination. "You still want to go with me? I can take you back to town."

"W.H. Ingram isn't the first artist to reinvent him or herself after a life-altering event, and I can't think of a single one who didn't come out on the other side as a better artist."

She glanced at the narrow lane leading off the main road. "Cecil Hawthorne and Jessica Blackwell didn't only damage one artist's career. Their dishonesty hurt the entire art community. So yeah, I'm in. Let's do this."

"Okay." Jake accelerated, made the turn onto the rutted roadway. "It's a good thing I rented a Jeep. Don't think a car would make it."

"These people must value their privacy."

"Fugitives usually do."

"And free-range chicken farmers," she countered as they came around a curve in the drive. A bunch of fowl pecked away in fenced pastureland as far as the eye could see.

"And free-range chicken farmers," Jake agreed. "Looks like the house and barn are up there." He pointed to the hint of a roofline in the distance.

"I'm sorry, but I don't see Cecil or Jessica as chicken farmers. Not even as a cover for whatever else they may be up to. I never knew them well, but they didn't strike me as the farmer type."

"You're probably right," he said, disappointment clear in his tone. "Just in case, we need to get a look at the owners." He drove on at a slow pace.

"Agreed."

As they made the last curve and the residence and barn came into view, a couple came out of the house. "What do you think? Could that be them?"

Sunny didn't need to get any closer. "No. Jessica is almost as tall as Cecil. That woman is shorter than me, and Cecil would have given anything to grow hair like that man has. He was very vocal about going bald early in life."

"He didn't shave his head?"

"Nope. Completely bald, naturally."

"Huh."

There was no place to turn around, so it was back down the drive or continue to the parking area between the house and barn. "You stay in the car. I'll play the lost tourist, and then we'll get out of here."

Sunny studied the young couple as Jake got out, asked them directions to the town where they'd spent the night. The farmers graciously set him on the right path. She smiled as he tipped his imaginary hat to them and returned to the Jeep.

He turned the vehicle around, waved goodbye, then they were headed toward the road once again. He propped an elbow on the door, rubbing his temple and forehead with his raised hand. "Not them," he said, his voice laced with disappointment.

"No. Not them."

He'd been off in his own world since leaving the farm, driving by rote. If not for Sunny's helpful reminders of where to turn, heaven only knew where they would have ended up. Arriving in town, they sat at the stop sign at the corner of Main and Maple until another motorist pulled up behind them and honked.

"Shit." Jake punched the gas, turned onto Main Street. He parked in front of the diner and they both got out. "I need a minute. Some caffeine and a sweet roll wouldn't be amiss, either. How about you?"

"I'll pass on the sweet roll. I'm still pretty full from breakfast, but coffee sounds good."

They sat at the counter. A different server from the one they'd seen earlier approached. "Morning, folks." Her smile seemed genuine and friendly. "New in town or passing through?"

"Passing through," Sunny responded. "I guess you know everyone in these parts?"

The woman nodded then reached for the coffee carafe behind her on the warmer. She held it up. "Regular?"

Jake flipped his mug over. Sunny followed suit and watched as the waitress filled both cups. "Not many new people around here. Mostly the old folks. They raise their kids. The kids move off to the city as soon as they can. Most don't come back."

Sunny fished the photos of Cecil and Jessica out of her

purse. She held them out to the woman. She talked as she stirred creamer into her coffee. "We're trying to find some friends of ours who we lost touch with. Last I heard, they were looking for property in this area. We got to thinking about them a few weeks ago and took some vacation time. Thought we'd see some scenery and maybe locate them."

CHAPTER NINE

Jake guzzled his coffee while Sunny did her thing. He had to hand it to her. She proved to be a first-rate actor. Marge, their server, bought her stupid story, hook, line, and sinker. She studied the photos before handing them back.

"The woman looks familiar, but I never seen the guy before. I'd remember his bald head, but I guess he could have been wearing a cap. Lots do around here. No manners, if you get my drift. Just sit there with their hat on like this is a barn." She topped off their mugs. "I could be mistaken about the woman. Is she a model or something?"

"No." Sunny tucked the photos away then added another thimble of cream to her mug before taking a sip. "She's an agent. Works mostly with artists. Or she did. Don't know what either of them are doing now. I think they'd both reached their burnout point, needed to try something different."

"We get a lot of city slickers out this way. Think they want to be farmers until they figure out how much work it is then they hightail it back to civilization. Some farms around here have changed hands a half dozen times in the last decade."

It occurred to Jake they were looking for the needle in the proverbial haystack. This close to the city, people came and went as if the freeway exit were a revolving door. People like Marge kept track of all the comings and goings. If a person, or persons, needed a place to hide out, this wasn't it. He drained his mug, tossed a twenty-dollar bill on the counter, and stood. "You ready to hit the road, sweetheart?"

Sunny stood, smiled at Marge. "Thanks for everything. It's been nice talking to you."

The older woman scooped their dirty coffee mugs into a tub beneath the counter then picked up the twenty. "You're welcome. Wish I could have helped you find your friends." She waved the currency in the air. "I'll get your change."

Jake hurried toward the door, Sunny on his heels. "Keep it." He pushed open the door. Heat and humidity smacked them in the face, making him wish he could stay indoors the rest of the day.

"You left a generous tip for two cups of coffee and a lot of talk."

Jake popped the door locks. They climbed in. Jake cranked the engine and set the air conditioner to full blast before fastening his seat belt. "She has the gift of gab, but it was probably the most enlightening conversation ever."

"How do you figure?" Sunny adjusted air vents to blow right on her then snapped her seat belt in place. "She didn't recognize Cecil or Jessica."

"She might have remembered Jessica from when she was here with Will, but that's irrelevant. The woman knows everyone here. She's a walking, talking history of every person who's moved in or out of this area for decades."

"I don't understand how her busybody tendencies are relevant at all."

Jake programmed the GPS for Callicoon before backing out of the parking space. "Listening to her, it occurred to me if someone was trying to disappear, this wasn't the place to do it. Too many people like Marge. Busybodies who have no problem sticking their nose in other people's business. Wherever Jessica and Cecil are, it's someplace where they could settle in with no one paying them much mind."

"Based on your assumption, they're probably still in the city. People move all the time. No one pays them any mind. You can live next door to someone for years and never have a conversation with them. You might not even see them. Ever."

"Exactly. I've been thinking like a guy from a small town. Thinking they'd go someplace remote. Marge changed my way of thinking."

"Then why are we going to Callicoon?"

"Because New York City is the largest city in the nation. If Cecil and Jessica are there, we'll never find them without help. Our best hope is Mr. McClelland. I got the impression he didn't leave Hawthorne's employ under the best of circumstances. He might know something. A connection we don't know about. A friend. Relative. Someone or someplace Cecil might go to hole up. And he might be willing to talk."

"You have a knack for this."

"Detective work?" Jake shook his head. "I'm a rank amateur."

"Don't sell yourself short. You're thinking this through, examining all angles. You're probably right about them being in the city, though I never would have reached the same conclusion based on what Marge told us. I guess that's what makes you an excellent lawyer."

"I'm an excellent lawyer because I hate to lose. No other reason."

❧

The bitterness in his voice rocked her back. "I sense a story here. Don't you enjoy what you do?" Silence sat between them like a mute hitchhiker, but Sunny refused to let the subject rest. "Well, tell me this. If you weren't a lawyer, what would you be?"

More silence. According to the GPS, a long stretch of road lay ahead before their next turn.

She tried a different tact. "I wanted to be a teacher."

Jake's gaze landed on her for a brief second then switched to the road again. "How did you end up owning a gallery instead?"

"This isn't about me, Jake Ingram. Answer my question and I'll tell you my sob story."

"What was your question again?"

"I sensed you don't want to be a lawyer, so I asked what you would be if you could be anything you wanted."

"You promise you won't laugh?"

"Promise."

"I wanted to be a writer. A novelist."

"So, why aren't you?"

He sighed, buying time to gather his thoughts. He'd told no one about his dream to become a writer. What would have been the point? His dad had mapped out his life for him, and Jake hadn't been able to say no to his plans. "My dad was a lawyer. He wanted—no—expected me to follow in his footsteps. I wasn't given a choice in the matter. I won't say I was opposed to becoming a lawyer. I figured it would provide me a decent living and allow me to get out from under my dad's thumb until the day came when I could break out of the mold and do what I wanted. That day never came."

"Why not? I don't understand what's keeping you from writing. Most of the writers I know—remember, I grew up in L.A. where everyone and their landlord thinks they can write a screenplay—have a regular job and write at night or in the morning before work. Where there's a will, there's a way."

Jake's derisive laugh filled the vehicle. "I guess you nailed the real problem. I lost the will."

"How did you end up with your own practice in your hometown?"

"I inherited it from my dad. There wasn't enough business for me to work with him right out of law school, so I got on with a firm in Houston. Learned a lot there. Found out I'm a decent litigator. I thought about writing, as you say, at night or weekends. Then Dad died, and I stepped into his shoes. Took over right where he left off. Lived in the same house I grew up in for years until I finally realized I wasn't going anywhere anytime soon. I bought a piece of land out on the lake and built myself a house. Big one with an office and a pool. I even built a pool house I imagined would become my writing cave."

"What happened?"

"Will was in New York. Rick was in the service. He spent a lot of time in the Middle East. My head wasn't in the right place, I guess. I worried about both of them, constantly. Instead of a novel, I was writing wills and handling divorces day in and day out. I'd get home at night, and the worry would creep in. Between worrying all night long and the boring-as-hell day job, whatever creativity I once possessed vanished. Sucked right out of me."

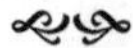

Jake clamped his jaw tight. What the hell came over him? Telling a virtual stranger his deepest, darkest secret?

The thought gave him pause. Was Sunny a stranger? He'd experienced his share of hookups with casual acquaintances and women he'd met at functions and bars. He'd never, not once, been inclined to tell them anything personal, much less reveal his most closely held secret. Even his brothers didn't know he'd always wanted to be a writer, and they knew him better than anyone on the planet. Except, perhaps, Sunny Sheldon.

He'd felt a connection to the pseudo-celebrity/gallery owner from the first moment he'd met her. A connection like no other. He'd thought it was a physical response to a beautiful woman, but if that was all it was, distance should have put an end to it. Two thousand miles and weeks later, he still woke in the middle of the night with a raging hard-on and memories of her fresh in his mind.

Those wake-up calls were the reason he returned to New York. He could have paid the private investigator to follow up on every lead. Doing it himself was nothing more than an excuse to see Sunny again—to find out if his dreams could somehow become reality.

He risked a glance at the woman in the passenger seat. She'd grown silent following his latest confession. Sitting there in her summer blouse and shorts, her hair pulled back in a high ponytail, her makeup the barest minimum, she took his breath away.

He wished he could say he was sorry the chicken farmers weren't the lowlifes who swindled Will out of a fortune, but he'd be lying if he did. As soon as he found Cecil and Jessica, he'd have no reason to stay in New York. His time with Sunny would end, and he wasn't ready to let her go. Not yet. The craving for her would go away sometime. Wouldn't it?

Desire would run its natural course in a few more days. The sex would lose its spark. It always did. No woman held his attention for long. He ignored the part of his brain reminding him he'd thought time and distance would help. Sunny was an anomaly. One his logical mind would eventually figure out and tire of.

"I'm sorry you didn't get to follow your own path in life."

Her words startled him out of his musings. He glanced her way. Their gazes met. Something in the depth of her eyes made him grip the steering wheel until his knuckles ached. It was either hang on tight or reach for her. The need to touch her, to ease the pain he sensed lurking below the surface was as real as his next breath.

Jerking his attention to the road ahead, he ground out, "Well, thanks, but shit happens." They rode in silence for a while then he asked, "So, you wanted to be a teacher? What happened to your dream?"

Gaze focused on the road ahead, she chuckled. "You've forgotten who my dad is?"

She said it like her dad's fame explained everything. Jake risked a glance her way. "No, but I don't see what his celebrity has to do with you not becoming a teacher."

She rolled her eyes at him. "I double majored in

college—art history and secondary education, got my degree, but to get a teaching credential, you have to complete a semester of student-teaching. Basically, an internship under an experienced educator. I got my assignment, showed up to the school for my first day, and ran into a wall of reporters. The principal asked me to leave and not come back." She shrugged. "It was a wake-up call for me. My grandmother left me her brownstone in New York. I knew celebrities who'd moved there, and they sang its praises. They could walk the sidewalks, eat in restaurants, do as they pleased without being harassed all the time by paparazzi. So, I packed up and relocated to New York."

"Why didn't you complete your student-teaching in New York?"

"Like you, I guess I lost my will to teach. Instead, I put my art history education to use and opened Sunnyside Gallery. I'm sure you've guessed; I don't need an income. Besides the brownstone, my grandmother left me a sizeable trust fund. My dad set one up for me, too. Dealing in art is something to do. Keeps me from going nuts, and I like to think I help up-and-coming artists."

"Like my brother."

"Yes. I've seen a lot of talent come through my gallery. Some are more talented than others. Your brother hit the top of my list early on and remains there. He's really good. I hope you realize how special he is."

"I do. I'm not an expert or art history major, but I know when something moves me. I'm excited to see what he comes up with once he gets past what they did to him. He seems…" Jake thought for a moment. "He seems older. Wiser. If that makes any sense?"

"It does. He has more emotions, more depth of character to draw upon. He's experienced more of life—albeit a sad and sorry side of life—but life nonetheless."

"I think it forced him to look inside himself for the first time. See who he really is. I hope the insight comes out in his new works because the world needs to see what an amazing person he is."

"I agree."

Silence filled the cab, except for the hum of the tires and the occasional road hazard warning from the navigation app. Jake appreciated the time to absorb what Sunny had revealed about herself. There were layers to her personality he hadn't expected. She was a giver, and she possessed a kind heart. He'd seen her acting ability at the diner and knew she could put on a performance when she wanted to, but he didn't think she was pretending now. Maybe she was a better actor than she claimed. He couldn't know for sure, but his gut told him the woman who'd given up her dream of teaching was as genuine as they came. A rare thing in his book.

"You getting hungry? I'm thinking we should try to find some grub."

Sunny's laughter filled the cab and lit a match to Jake's libido. He was coming to realize it didn't take much where she was concerned to get him stirred up. "Grub? Don't look now, but your hillbilly is showing, Counselor."

"Just be glad I left my camo at home."

"Seriously? You have camo gear? The real kind, not the stuff people buy in high-priced boutiques and think they look cool?"

"You don't?" he asked, deadpan.

"No! Why would I?"

"I don't know. For all I know, you hunt your own meat and have a basement full of vegetables you canned yourself."

God, he loved to hear her laugh. Would keep up the silly banter forever just to see her smile. He fought the urge to pull off the road and make her smile for a different reason.

"Never been hunting, and, other than an experiment I did for the science fair in second grade, I've never grown anything in my life. I don't even have house plants." She held out both hands. "Two brown thumbs."

"Confession. I don't own any camo. My brother, Rick, used to have a complete wardrobe of the stuff. Liked to go hunting. That was before he joined the Navy. Since he's been home, I haven't seen him wear anything but jeans and T-shirts."

"Lost his taste for hunting?"

"I don't know. He's not much of a talker. Never was."

"You're an interesting family. A lawyer/wannabe writer, an artist, and a warrior."

"I don't know about interesting, but we are a family. We look out for each other."

"Must be nice."

Jake picked up on the wistful tone in her voice. "You don't enjoy being an only child?"

"I loved it when I was a kid, but as an adult I think it would be fun to have someone close to my age to share things with, to talk to."

He often thought having siblings was overrated, but, looking at it from her perspective, he had to admit he never felt alone. Not even when his brothers were off leading their own lives. He'd always known they were there. A phone call away, most of the time, and they had his back, no matter what. "I've got two brothers. I can loan you one."

Her smile and soft laughter wrecked him.

"Thanks, but I'm okay. I've got friends, and my parents."

CHAPTER TEN

Jake's silly offer to loan one of his brothers was sweet, but she didn't want Will or Rick. She wanted Jake. She tried to tell herself this was a physical thing. Great sex clouding her mind. But it was more than just sex. Jake Ingram was getting under her skin a little more with each thing he revealed about himself. No doubt he'd make a fabulous writer once he pursued his dream. He was an excellent storyteller, captivating her with his tales of growing up in a small Texas town as they put the Manhattan skyline farther behind them. And with each mile, she fell a little harder for him.

This would not end well for her. Jake would probably go on his merry way. Put a few extra notches—okay—a lot of extra notches in his bedpost when he got home in. He'd move on to some other woman and forget all about her. A man like him wouldn't be lonely for long. But the thought of being with anyone else creeped Sunny out. Maybe in a few months? Perhaps the memories would fade, and she'd see the flaws in the man. Realize how silly she'd been to put him on a pedestal and slap a label on him—*the one*. He couldn't be. He lived a different life from hers in another state, for crying out loud!

It was the sex. She'd never had better. Which, admittedly, wasn't saying much, given her lack of partners recently.

If it wasn't the sex, it had to be his Southern drawl. Always present but more so when passion ruled him, as if he had better things to do than modulate his voice. Oh, and the things he could do. Which brought her right back to the superb sex.

Ugh! Didn't she just prove her own point. She wasn't falling in love with the man. She was in a sex stupor. Once he went home, the pheromone fog would lift, and she'd be back to normal.

Translation: she'd be alone.

"Hey."

She plastered a smile on her face then turned to the man who occupied all her thoughts these days. "Hey, yourself."

"I'm starving. Want to check the mapping app for a place to eat?"

"Sure." She grabbed her phone from the cup holder. After an exhaustive search, she grimaced. "There's not much to choose from. No fast food of any kind. A few mom-and-pop places. There's one in Narrowsburg that sounds okay. Want to try it?"

"I should have had a piece of pie with my coffee back there to tide me over." His stomach growled as if agreeing with his assessment. "Plug in the address so we don't waste time getting lost."

Sunny chuckled then keyed the information into the navigation system. "Do we have a place to spend the night?"

Jake tapped the steering wheel with his index finger, his gaze fixed on the road and the enormous travel trailer trudging along ahead of them. "Uh. That would be a no. Want to see what you can find?"

"Where are we going, again? Calhoun?"

"Callicoon. I think it's close to Narrowsburg."

"Never heard of it."

"They have a post office."

"That's reassuring."

Following the automated directions, they eventually

pulled into the parking lot of the eating establishment which turned out to be connected to a gas station via a convenience store. Potholes and weeds warred for top billing with gravel. An abandoned rail line ran behind the structure.

"I think that's a grocery store." Sunny pointed to a metal building across the street. "If this doesn't work out, we can see if they have a deli."

Jake stretched his arms above his head. She watched, her body heating as memories of the way he looked beneath his clothes came to mind. He propped one foot then the other on the bumper for some leg stretches. "I'm thinking it might be wise to have a stash of snacks and some water bottles in the car. The scarcity of services in this area reminds me of parts of Texas. I didn't expect this area to be so remote."

Together, they approached the diner. A server wearing jeans and a T-shirt, an apron tied around her waist, and a towel draped over one shoulder waved to them. "Take any seat you want. I'll be right with you."

The only other patron, a man wearing dirt-streaked jeans and a sweat-soaked shirt attacked a burger and fries at the Formica-topped breakfast counter. They chose a booth next to the plate-glass window overlooking the parking lot. The hard wooden seats didn't invite patrons to linger over endless cups of coffee, though an assortment of pies in a refrigerated case on the wall behind the counter suggested dessert might be in order. After checking out the ads from local businesses printed on the paper placemats, they examined the menus from the condiment rack. By the time the lone waitress came around to take their order, they'd made their selections.

"I'll have the cheeseburger and fries." Sunny returned her menu to the rack next to the wall. "And a diet soda, please."

The woman didn't bother to write the order down. "How you want your burger cooked, hon?"

"Medium-well, please."

She turned her attention to Jake. He ordered the same but went with iced tea. "Be right back with your drinks." True to her word, she plunked the plastic glasses and paper-wrapped straws on the table before disappearing through the swinging door leading to the kitchen.

Jake dumped a packet of artificial sweetener in his glass then stirred it with a straw. He took a sip and grimaced. "It's times like this I really miss Texas."

Sunny smiled. "That bad?"

"Tastes like horse piss."

"You don't really know what horse piss tastes like, do you?"

He shoved the offending beverage as far away as possible on the small table. "No, but I can imagine. Want to try it? See what you think?"

"Nope." She took a long draw on her straw. "I'll stick with my soda." She held the glass out. "Want some?"

"Nah. I'll have her bring me one when she comes back." He returned his attention to the placemat ads. "We need to find a hotel for tonight."

"Good luck finding a room." They both straightened to allow the server to set plates on the table. "There's a festival in town this weekend. Even the campgrounds are full."

"What about Callicoon?" Jake adjusted the plate in front of him to suit him. "That's close to here, isn't it?"

"It's north of here a few miles. There's a small, historic hotel there, but I wouldn't count on finding a room. If you're looking for one of those chain hotels, you'll be driving to Scranton for the night."

"Pennsylvania?" Sunny couldn't keep the horror out of her voice.

The woman rolled her eyes. "Hon, Pennsylvania is just across the river. Scranton is about an hour's drive unless you get behind a sightseer then it could take longer."

"You get many sightseers?" Jake asked.

"Plenty. People come up to fish the Delaware River. See the bald eagles. Camp. Lots of summer communities in these parts. Like I said, RiverFest is this weekend. Lots of people in town for the event. Craft vendors. Tourists. Figured you were here for the festivities."

"No, though I wish I'd known about the festival beforehand. I would have planned to stay awhile." Jake graced her with a hundred-megawatt smile. "Appreciate the info."

"Visitor information is on the house. You two enjoy your burgers. Is there anything else I can get you?"

"Nope. We're good."

Sunny glanced at Jake's untouched beverage then back to him as the waitress sauntered off. "What about your iced tea?"

Stuffing a french fry in his mouth, Jake shrugged. "I'll grab a water bottle later. I doubt it's her fault the tea tastes like horse piss." He grabbed the ketchup container, squirted the stuff all over his fries.

Sunny reached for the dispenser. When he handed it over, she carefully moved things around on her plate then filled the space with the sweet condiment. "Is that a Texas thing?" She motioned to his doused fries. "Drowning your potatoes before you eat them?"

He swirled another crispy slice through the sauce then popped it in his mouth. He pointed to the tidy dot of the sweet condiment nestled off to the side of her plate. "Is that a New York thing? Isn't the idea to get the ketchup on the fries?"

"Yes, but they get all soggy if you dump it on top of them."

He held up a limp fry coated with red goo. "Don't see what's wrong with my method." He opened his mouth, crammed the potato in, chewing with obvious satisfaction. "Mm-mm. Good stuff."

Shaking her head, she abandoned the argument over french fry etiquette for their previous topic. "I don't know about you, but I don't want to spend the night in your Jeep."

"I wasn't planning on driving to Scranton, but if we have to, we will." He took a big bite of his burger. Grabbing a napkin from the dispenser on the table, he dabbed the corners of his mouth as he swallowed. "Let's see if we can locate McClelland first. If he has a lead, we might want to head in a different direction before we call it a night."

"Sounds like a plan. How far are we from his house?"

"Half an hour? That's my best guess. Every road we've been on since we left the interstate has been narrow and winding. Not to mention full of potholes."

"So I've noticed." She pushed her plate away. "Why don't we get gas then go across the street to the grocery store? We can stock up on snacks and drinks for the road."

"Sounds like a plan to me. I'd bet they have a Styrofoam cooler for sale. That and a bag of ice and we're good."

Jake paid the bill. While he pumped the gas, she plugged their next destination into the navigation system. "You were right. We're only about a half hour from his house," she said as he climbed into the driver's seat.

"Best news I've heard all day." He pulled away from the pump. Traffic, mostly giant pickups towing even bigger campers, made it difficult to cross to the grocery store, but patience won out. The outside of the store didn't look like much, but the inside was brightly lit. The floors were clean and the shelves well stocked. Jake spied a stack of Styrofoam coolers near the registers. He tossed one in their cart. "Get whatever you think we need. I don't want to be stuck on one of these roads after dark with no place to sleep and nothing to eat. If we have grub, we can power through until we get someplace that has accommodations."

"I really, really don't want to sleep in the car."

"Me, either." He walked beside her, pushing the cart. "I'm holding out for a safe, clean room with a giant tub and a king-sized bed."

Sunny moaned. "A nice long soak sounds like heaven."

"Then let's get a move on. The sooner we find McClelland, the sooner we both get what we want."

CHAPTER ELEVEN

With their new cooler stocked with water bottles and snacks, they resumed the drive. Jake liked trees as much as the next guy, but as they wound back and forth through the forested Catskill mountains, he longed for the wide-open spaces of North Texas. If it weren't for the opportunity to spend time with Sunny, he would have gladly handed this part of the investigation over to the private investigator. He hoped Hawthorne's former PR guru was at home and would willingly give up any information he had so they could get out of the mountains before it got dark.

According to the GPS, they were less than five miles from their destination when they came upon a construction crew doing road repairs. One of the two lanes was closed. A stout woman wearing a reflective vest and holding a stop sign stood in the roadway, stopping their progress while oncoming traffic streamed by at a crawl. Jake put the Jeep in Park and took his foot off the brake. "Wonder how many potholes this stretch of road had if it gets repaired while the others we've been on don't warrant any attention."

"It must have been one giant pothole," Sunny agreed. "But at least they're repairing something."

Jake tapped the steering wheel. Something had been bothering him since they'd left the chicken farmer's place earlier that morning. The closer they got to McClelland's house, the more it bugged him. Changing the subject in the middle of a conversation was a cheap lawyer trick to catch a witness off guard. He hated pulling it out now, but he wanted an honest answer or, at the very least, an honest response. "Do you know Ross McClelland?"

Sunny snapped her head around to meet his gaze. "No. I think I may have talked with him on the phone once several years ago, but he worked behind the scenes as most PR people do. Like my PR person does."

At her vehement denial, a weight lifted from his chest. Everything he'd learned about Sunny Sheldon pointed to her being squeaky clean and honest in her business dealings. The lawyer in him found it hard to believe anyone could be as perfect as she seemed, but the more time he spent with her, the more he trusted her. And the more he wanted her. He couldn't seem to keep his hands off her. Reaching across the console, he took her hand, squeezed it gently. "Just wanted to know if you'd recognize him," he lied.

Sunny returned the hand squeeze. "I doubt I would. If I ever saw him, I didn't know who he was. It's possible we were in the same place at the same time. Some gallery openings are enormous affairs. Others, not so much."

"So, he might recognize you?"

She shrugged. "It's possible. Probably more likely than me recognizing him. I am a public figure—albeit a minor one. Couple that with owning a gallery, and you can see how the two might make me more visible than your average person in the art world."

The traffic controller turned their stop sign around so it read, *proceed with caution* then waved them to the open lane. He fell in behind the line of cars ahead of them. Once past the construction, he swerved back into the right lane, and they continued to their destination. "I think this is it." Jake put on his turn signal and slowed to make the left turn.

"Wow! What a house!" Sunny gawked at the Victorian set atop a gentle slope.

Jake concurred. According to the private investigator, the house sat on close to 100 acres of mixed-use property. About half had been cleared for farming over a century ago, while they'd left the rest untouched. The house and acreage had been in the McClelland family for four generations. Ross was the last living descendant of the original settlers. "It seems like a lot for a single guy. Especially one as old as he is."

"How old is he?"

"According to the investigator I hired, he's 72 and in failing health."

"Someone must help him keep all this up. A lawn this size doesn't mow itself, and the house looks to be in remarkable shape." She pointed to an outbuilding revealed as they got closer. "You don't see barns like that every day. This place is gorgeous!"

Jake followed the paved drive around to the back of the house where a late-model Lexus sat next to an older GMC pickup with more rust than paint. He pulled up short of the vehicles and cut the engine. Before they could exit the car, an old gentleman appeared on the porch, pushed the screen door open. He pointed a double-barreled shotgun at them like he knew what to do with it.

"Not the greeting I expected," Jake said.

Sunny's voice shook. "Let's leave before he shoots us."

"Give me a minute." Jake opened his door and stepped out, hands raised. "Name's Jake Ingram. Came all the way from Texas to talk to Ross McClelland." He stepped toward the man. "Would that be you, sir? I promise, I just want a minute of your time."

"State your business."

"My brother is W. H. Ingram. Does the name ring any bells?"

"You should have led with that." The gun barrel dipped slightly. Jake took it as a friendly sign and approached with caution. "Still don't see what you want with me."

"I'm hoping you can help me locate your former employer, Cecil Hawthorne. He stole a year's worth of my brother's work. I'm trying to get the paintings back."

"Goddamnit. Hawthorne always was a piece of shit." McClelland rested the weapon next to him inside the screened porch. He squinted at the Jeep. "Who's with you?"

"Sunny Sheldon. She owns Sunnyside Gallery."

"I know who she is. You two come in and tell me what this is all about." The door banged shut behind him as he retreated into the house.

Jake returned to the Jeep, leaned in. "Doesn't sound like he much cares for Hawthorne."

"No, it doesn't." Sunny released her seat belt. "You think it's safe to go in?"

"Yeah. Can't blame the old guy for being cautious."

"Guess not, but at the first sign of trouble, I'm calling 9-1-1." She held up her cell phone.

Jake smiled at her feisty attitude. "I don't think you'll need to call reinforcements, but if having a phone in your hand makes you feel safer, by all means…" He waited for her to join him before following McClelland into the house.

He found the old man in the kitchen, pouring hot water from an ancient kettle into three generous sized mugs. He handed one to Jake then carried the other two to a scarred oak table in the center of the eat-in kitchen. There was nothing modern about this farmhouse kitchen. Everything from the dated appliances to the worn linoleum and scarred Formica countertops screamed authenticity circa 1950. The cabinets themselves were probably original to the house, judging from the way the white paint on them had aged. Jake instantly thought of Hank Travis and the exorbitant amount of money he'd spent to hide a modern kitchen behind a similar façade. Given a choice, Jake would take the warmth of this one over sleek and modern anytime.

"Have a seat." He set the extra cup in front of Sunny then sat across from her. Jake sat next to her. "Pick your poison." McClelland opened an intricately carved wooden box in the center of the table. "Got any kind of tea you can imagine in there. Sugar is on the table. Milk's in the fridge."

Jake preferred his tea sweet and iced, but he wasn't about to decline the man's offer. He'd drink the horse-piss from the diner before he'd insult the old man. He waited for Sunny to choose from the well-stocked supply then grabbed the same. Following her lead, he opened the small packet and dunked the tea bag into his mug. Their host made his selection, adding a generous scoop of sugar to his mug.

"Sorry about the greeting. I don't get many visitors."

"Don't blame you for being cautious. You live here alone?" Jake asked.

"I do. I grew up in this house. It was a different world then. You could trust your neighbors. Used to, you could trust your employer, too." He dunked his tea bag several times then brought the mug to his lips for a taste. "Cecil Hawthorne used to be an honest man. He changed once he met that woman. After she got her hooks in him, he lost every scrap of integrity he ever possessed. I decided it was time to retire shortly after they got together. Sold everything but my art collection and moved out here to spend my golden years in peace."

"You have a lovely home," Sunny said, glancing around at the clean but outdated kitchen. "I'd love to see the rest of the house."

Humor flashed in the old man's eyes. "You want to see my art collection," he stated, flatly. "Don't worry. I'll let you see it before you go."

Jake raised an eyebrow at Sunny. "What? He spent a lifetime in the New York art world. He worked with the best up-and-coming artists in the world. I'd be a fool to pass up the chance to see what he collected."

"She's right." Ross raised his mug, took a sip. "I bought as much as I could afford. Lived in a crappy fifth-floor walkup so I could afford to buy what I liked. I have two of your brother's paintings. His early stuff."

"I'd love to see them," Jake said, honestly. He'd missed a lot during the years his brother lived in the city. Missed seeing him grow as an artist. "But first, what can you tell us about

Cecil Hawthorne?"

"I've been out of touch with the art scene for several years now. What did he do?"

Jake filled him in on the crime his former employer perpetrated against Will. "I'm not only Will's brother, I'm his attorney," he concluded. "The bank made good on the funds they let slip through their hands. Now, I'm trying to get the paintings back."

"You don't think Hawthorne destroyed them?"

Sunny jumped in, regaling the older gentleman with the reasons they believed Cecil and Jessica still had the paintings.

McClelland got up, refilled his mug from the still-warm kettle. Jake and Sunny waited for him to respond. After a few minutes, he looked up from stirring sugar into his tea. "I'm sorry to hear William has suffered so at the hands of a man I once thought of as a friend." The older man locked gazes with Jake. "Your brother has a rare talent. I don't know if it helps, but I think Cecil was jealous of his talent."

"What makes you say so?"

"Most people involved in the art world fall into one of two categories. Either they create art, or they wish they could. The wishers work behind the scenes. They own or work in galleries"—he nodded at Sunny who acknowledged his guess with a nod of her own—"or they become patrons. I fell into both. I worked in public relations for several galleries over the years, and I did what I could to support artists I believed in by purchasing their work whenever I could. I sacrificed to save enough to buy the pieces I admired the most. Cecil was too fond of keeping up appearances to be a patron. Most of the commissions he made from sales went to feeding his taste for expensive things. The trendiest loft apartment. Tailored suits. Lavish parties. Expensive vacations. His bank accounts were always scraping bottom because of it, so it doesn't surprise me he tapped into someone else's accounts."

"Why would he steal the paintings though?" Jake asked. "He has to know selling them will put him at risk."

"I wouldn't put it past him to sell them at some point.

Your brother acquired quite a few loyal patrons, and anyone with an appreciation for fine art could see the value in owning one of his canvases." He took a sip of his tea. "But I think the theft goes back to my first statement."

"Jealousy," Sunny supplied.

McClelland tipped his head to her. "He hid it well, but sometimes, in private, he'd let it slip. He wouldn't come out and say he was jealous, but he'd pick an artist's work apart with a bitterness you couldn't mistake for anything else."

"He did that to Will's work?"

"Oh yes. He was harsh when it came to anything by W.H. Ingram." Ross cleared his throat and stood. "I want to show you something."

They followed him down a long hallway lined with paintings on both walls. Most were what Jake thought of as modern. Blocks of color, distorted images, swirls of paint he couldn't make heads or tails of. McClelland led them past a magnificent stairway at the front of the house to what Jake's grandma would have called a parlor. Landscapes of every size and description lined the walls. Hanging in a place of honor above the fireplace mantel was a painting Jake immediately recognized as his brother's work.

Ross flicked a switch, illuminating the painting in a soft light. The familiar scene took Jake back over a dozen years. He swallowed past the lump in his throat and willed the moisture in his eyes to stay put.

Beside him, Sunny squeezed his hand. "It's the three of you, isn't it?"

"Yeah. Down by the creek." Will captured the moment perfectly. Three boys, staggered in age, dressed in their Sunday best, sat on the bank of the creek, their backs to the artist, their heads and shoulders dipped in sorrow. "That was right after our mother's funeral. We got in trouble later for leaving the house, but we needed to get away from all the people and process. We sat there for hours. Didn't speak a word, if I recall correctly. Eventually, Rick stood up. Will and I got up and followed him home. We never discussed it.

Never mentioned those stolen hours again, but I remember it like it was yesterday."

"I fell in love with the painting the moment I saw it." Ross's face tilted up at the artwork. "It's full of emotion. From the set of the boy's shoulders to the stillness of the willow trees and the ominous clouds on the horizon. I didn't know who the subjects were, but I related to them immediately. We've all known sorrow. The kind that reaches down to the marrow of our bones."

"He captured the day exactly how I remember it." Jake pointed to a clump of flowers off to one side. "The bluebonnets were starting to bloom. My mother loved them. She'd take us walking along the riverbank every year to see them. We went back when they'd gone to seed and collected as many seeds as we could fit in our pockets. The three of us planted them over her grave."

"What a beautiful story." Sunny squeezed his hand so hard he winced.

Jake took a deep breath, let it out. "If you ever want to sell it, call me."

The old man nodded. "I won't tell you the things Cecil said about the painting, but none of it was good. Where he resented your brother's talent, I rejoiced in it. There isn't a soul on the planet who wouldn't be moved by that painting. Unfortunately, it moved Cecil too much, in a bad way."

"Do you have any idea where he and Jessica could be?"

"I might." He led them to the dining room where another of Will's paintings hung in a place of honor. This one captured the spirit of the Fourth of July holiday in downtown Willowbrook from the patriotic bunting on the gazebo in the park to the families beneath the ancient oak trees, playing, picnicking. He captured the details down to scraps of busted balloons lying discarded in the grass, a little boy standing over it, tears streaking down his cheeks at the loss of his toy.

Jake studied the painting for a minute before he spoke, his voice thick with emotion. "That's Rick. Our baby brother. He was almost two then." He pointed to a couple on a plaid picnic blanket. "Those are our parents. And see"—he pointed out two older boys making their way through the crowd with a shiny red balloon in tow—"that's me and Will. Rick cried at the drop of a hat when he was little. His balloon popped. Will and I couldn't stand it, so we got him another one from the vendor. I'd forgotten all about that."

"Thanks for telling me the story. I'd never connected the two boys in the background with the crying baby in the foreground. It reminded me of my childhood. Callicoon used to have a big Fourth of July celebration. Now, not so much. All the young people have moved away. Nothing but old folks living here these days."

"Thanks for showing me the paintings. It makes me more determined to get the others back."

Sunny was eager to see the rest of the man's collection, so they wandered the rooms and hallways for an hour or more before returning to the kitchen where they sat around the table. "Cecil, despite his expensive tastes, grew up in a working-class neighborhood in Scranton. His grandfather was a coal miner. His dad worked for the railroad, as I recall. The work was above ground, and a step in the right direction for the family, but it wasn't the life Cecil wanted for himself. He's an only child, so when his parents passed, he inherited their house in Scranton. Or maybe it was Wilkes-Barre." He waved the memory lapse away. "Anyway, he held on to the house. Why, I never knew. Maybe it was security in case everything went to shit, which it did if he resorted to stealing from an artist."

Jake drummed his fingers on the table. "Why hasn't anyone mentioned this before? I've had a private investigator looking for Hawthorne ever since Will told me what happened. The police are investigating, too. No one has mentioned a house in Pennsylvania."

"Probably because Hawthorne isn't his actual name." Ross shook his head. "I'm sorry. I assumed you already knew."

Sunny recovered from the shock first and asked, "What

is his real name?"

"Obediah Shupp, Jr. Named after his father. Don't know how that got overlooked. Everything was in his legal name—including the lease on the gallery."

Jake stood, pulled his cell phone from his pocket. "Excuse me. I need to make some phone calls. This changes everything."

CHAPTER TWELVE

Sunny shook her head. "I can't believe no one connected the dots."

"I can." Pushing away from the table, Ross got to his feet. "It's getting late. You should stay here tonight." He opened the vintage refrigerator. "I'll fix us something to eat."

"That's nice of you, but we should be going." She stood.

"Nonsense. Sit yourself down. I'll scare up something to eat then, if you really want to drive these back roads in the dark, you can go. Besides, it will take your fancy investigator a while to generate a report on Shupp. For all I know, Cecil could have sold the house in Pennsylvania years ago. He wouldn't have told me if he had."

Resolved to stay a little longer, Sunny resumed her seat. "You weren't close?"

"No. I was good at my job, so he kept me around, and I have an excellent eye for quality art, something he claimed to have but didn't, really. His lack of education was a detriment to his chosen profession. Like I said, he was a wannabe painter. His parents needed him to work, contribute to the household income, and he did until he graduated from high school. Then he took off for New York. He adopted his new name and worked his way up in the art world—all the way from gopher to gallery owner. Not bad for a guy with no formal instruction."

"No, not bad at all." Sunny finger traced the carvings on the antique tea chest as Ross chopped onions and tossed them on top of a lump of ground meat he'd dumped into a mixing bowl. "Why did you leave?"

"Hamburgers okay?" he asked. "We can grill 'em up pretty fast. Don't want to keep you two any longer than necessary if you're bent on getting out of here tonight."

Jake returned in time to hear the last part. "Are you fixing dinner?"

"We gotta eat, and in case you didn't notice, there aren't many restaurants out this way."

"Thanks." He leaned against the doorframe, his arms crossed over his chest. "Philip said he'd get right on it. We should have an address by morning."

"Jake, Mr. McClelland suggested we spend the night here. What do you think?"

"I think it sounds like a fantastic idea. I wasn't looking forward to driving the roads up here after dark." He turned his attention to the former public relations guru. "Are you sure we won't be an imposition?"

Ross waved a wooden spoon in the air. "Not at all. Stay as long as you want. Besides"—he glanced Sunny's way—"I'd like to catch up on what's been going on since I left."

Sunny smiled at the old man. "Hawthorne's actions rocked the industry. That's what's been going on. You didn't tell me why you quit when you did. What happened?"

Jake pulled out the chair next to Sunny and sat. Ross washed his hands then scooped up a handful of the meat mixture and squashed it into a rough patty then went to work on another one. Setting the finished patties aside, he sighed and wiped his hands on the dishrag he'd tucked into his waistband. With a sigh, he leaned against the counter facing them. "My life partner died. Frank and I were together for thirty-five years."

"I'm so sorry," Sunny said. "I didn't know."

"Thanks." He studied his shoes for a moment; when he

lifted his gaze to the two sitting at his table, the sheen of unshed tears glistened in his eyes. "Few knew about Frank. We led a quiet life. He worked on Wall Street but, like me, preferred to keep to himself. No parties for him. I only went to the ones necessary for my job. Frank knew less about art than Cecil, but he never discouraged me from collecting."

"I wondered how you afforded to amass a collection the size of yours." Jake sat back, drumming his fingers on the table. "I didn't buy your story about scraping by, saving to purchase art."

Ross returned to the meal preparation. "It was mostly true. Frank and I lived in a fifth-floor walkup. I lived there for over a decade before we met. When he moved in, he started paying most of our expenses which were nothing for him and a burden for me. His generosity allowed me to splurge on art. So, it wasn't actually a lie."

"Then he died," Sunny prompted.

Ross nodded. "Heart attack at the office. He was gone before I got to the hospital." He added the final patty to the plate with the others then scrubbed his hands at the sink. "He left me everything, which was quite a lot. He was good. Knew when to buy. When to sell. Said it was instinct. Anyway, I was in a bad place after he died. My heart wasn't in my work any longer. Then that Jessica woman started hanging around with Cecil. She hated me, and I hated her. So I retired. Came out here where there's room to hang all the paintings I've collected. What good's a collection if you can't enjoy it, right?"

Ross opened a drawer, pulled out a metal spatula. "I figure a Texan knows his way around a grill." He handed the long-handled tool off to Jake. "Mind doing the honors while I come up with side dishes?"

"Not at all." Jake took the plate of meat and the utensil. "How do you like yours?"

"Well-done. I'm old. Last thing I need is to catch E. coli from a burger."

"I hear you. Two well-done patties coming up. Sunny?

How do you like yours?"

"Medium-well?"

"Grill's that way." Ross pointed to the door they'd used when they first arrived. "Fancy one. Has a self-starter and a light so you can see what you're doing at night."

Jake disappeared out the back door. Sunny stood. "What can I do?"

"Set the table?" He ducked his head into the refrigerator, came out with a gigantic bowl covered in plastic wrap. "I made a macaroni salad yesterday. Never figured out how to make a single serving of the stuff." He placed the serving dish in the middle of the table, yanked the cover off, and stuck a big spoon in. "You'll be doing me a favor if you eat it all up."

Sunny got plates from the cabinet and silverware from a drawer. "I live alone, too. It's harder than it looks to cook for one person."

"Tell me about it. I don't mind leftovers, but after several days eating the same thing, I give up and toss it out."

"Do you ever think about moving back to the city?"

"Every time a stranger drives up and I have to get out the shotgun."

"Does that happen often?"

"Thankfully, no." Ross produced a bag of potato chips from a cabinet. After removing the clothes pin he'd used to secure the opening, he placed it beside the bowl of macaroni salad. "It's quiet out here. Exactly what I needed after losing Frank."

"Well, if you ever have the urge to visit some galleries, you're welcome to stay at my house. I have a brownstone on the Upper East Side. My grandmother left it to me," she added.

"Sounds swanky."

Sunny laughed. "Not hardly. It was a mess when I got it. I did some remodeling before I moved in, but it's far from fancy."

"I thought, with all the money your father has, you'd live in one of the modern high-rises."

"You know about my dad?"

"Doesn't everyone?" Ross snatched a chip from the bag. "It was common knowledge in the art community."

A sigh escaped her lips. "I suppose it is, though I try to keep my parentage quiet."

"You didn't want to go into acting?"

Sunny shook her head. "Nope. Plenty of opportunities came my way, but acting isn't my thing."

"I bet you could have any part you wanted." Ross abruptly stood. "Forgot the buns." He lifted the lid on an old-fashioned bread box. "Knew I had some." They joined the salad and chips on the table. He added a plate of lettuce leaves and tomato slices. Bottles of mustard and ketchup completed the meal.

"You're right about the divide in the art world." Sunny helped herself to a chip. "I dabble at painting. Never had the nerve to show the paintings to anyone. I've got enough of an eye to recognize my talent lies in identifying artistic talent in others."

"I'd like to see your work sometime."

She shook her head. "Oh, no, you wouldn't. Trust me. I've seen paint-by-numbers that were better."

"I'm sure it's not as bad as you think. It's the artist who thinks they're the best thing since Rembrandt that you have to watch out for. They have no self-awareness and don't appreciate being told their work stinks. The critical ones usually can't see their own talent. It takes a while to convince them otherwise."

She was still thinking about McClelland's statement when Jake came in bearing perfectly grilled hamburger patties. They took a minute to add lettuce, tomato, and pickles to their burgers then piled their plates with chips and homemade salad.

They chowed down for a few minutes then the old man broke the silence. "How's your brother doing? He's still painting, isn't he?"

Jake wiped grease from his lips with a paper napkin.

"Will is doing better. This whole thing spun him out for a while." He sipped the beer Ross provided. "Did you ever meet your replacement?"

"MacKenzie something or other? No, but I talked to her several times when she first took over. She was green but eager. Why?"

"Just wondering." Jake took another bite of his burger, chewed, and swallowed. "Thanks to Sunny, MacKenzie got a job in our town, working for our resident rock star who also is a friend of Sunny's. MacKenzie and Will are…dating, I guess you could say."

"Really? That's the definition of a small world."

Jake nodded. "She's the one who gave us your name."

"Did I get it wrong? I thought she was involved with Cecil. She never said as much, but I got that impression."

"You weren't wrong. Apparently, she knew nothing about his relationship with Jessica. She'd moved in with him. Thought they would get married. He left her high and dry, too. No job. No money to pay the rent on his loft. She was fortunate Sunny knew Hank was looking for a new PR person."

"She and your brother are a thing now. Huh." He sat back, popped a chip in his mouth. "Funny how things work out sometimes," he said, eyeing Jake and Sunny who spoke at once.

"Oh no. We aren't…"

"We're not…"

"Don't try to fool an old man. I saw you holding hands. Saw the way you look at each other. If I'm wrong, tell me and I'll direct you to separate rooms for the night. Otherwise, the guest room at the back of the house is yours. It has a private bath."

"It's new," Sunny said.

Ross gathered his plate and took it to the sink. "I'm just sayin'…something good might have come of this whole sordid affair."

Sunny offered another protest, but the old man was

having none of it. He waved off her comments before they got past her lips.

"I'm sure you kids are tired," Ross said, drying his hands. "You've had a long day. Let me show you to your room. I can clean this up later."

CHAPTER THIRTEEN

In the privacy of their room, Jake mulled over the possibility something lasting could come from the few days he'd spent with Sunny. No matter how he tried, he couldn't get past the fact they lived in two different states, far, far apart. She had her life in New York, and he had his in Texas. Even if he were willing to pick up and move halfway across the country, it wouldn't change the discontent weighing him down. He'd still need to make a living, and the law met those needs. Other than being with Sunny, which was a huge plus, he'd still be living a life he didn't want.

When she came out of the bathroom, wearing nothing but barely there panties and a slinky top that ended a couple of inches above her belly button, every thought but one flew out of his head. *Mine.* Need gripped him. Sunny Sheldon was quickly becoming an addiction he couldn't afford but had no intention of giving up. Not now, at least. Advancing on her, he framed her face in his hands, tilted her at the perfect angle, then crushed her lips with his.

Instinct drove them. They shed clothes in record time and came together like a summer storm, fast and anything but gentle. Moving over her, inside her, Jake knew he should take more care with her, but the primal urge to claim, to possess overrode everything else. Through every driving thrust, every savage nip, every possessive grip, Sunny was right there with him, her body moving against his, giving, taking, in equal measure. When she threw her head back, screamed his name, her inner walls grasping, Jake released the tether he held on his own pleasure. Jaw clamped tight, his entire being focused on their joined bodies, the orgasm began as a fireball in the small of his back and burned its way through his abdomen to spew from him in gut-wrenching spurts that stole his breath and all but stopped his heart.

He didn't know how long he'd lain on her, crushing her into the mattress with his sweaty weight. Rousing, he rolled off to the side. Arms thrown over his head, legs spread, he concentrated on bringing air into his lungs. "Are you okay?"

The answering affirmative hum eased his all-too familiar guilt at having taken her so hard. He really knew how to finesse a woman. He'd perfected the art of making love over the years, but with Sunny, everything he knew about what a woman liked vanished like smoke signals on a windy day.

He blew out a sharp breath. "We should have opened a window. I think I'm having a heat stroke."

Beside him, Sunny rolled to her side to face him. She rested a hand on his chest, her fingers tangling in the light mat of hair across his pecs. "I need another shower."

Jake reached for her, dragging her against him again. "Don't put images in my head. Please. I don't think I can take it." But it was too late. He could imagine her in the tiny enclosure, her body slick with soap, water cascading over her luscious curves. Desire stirred within. Jake groaned and, with one hand behind his head, reached for his cock with the other. "You're killing me, woman."

When her hand joined his, stroking his quickly hardening shaft, he cursed under his breath and rocked his hips in concert with their joint ministrations. Much more stimulation and he'd blow like a teenager in the movie theatre balcony.

"I've never been with someone like you," she said, a hint of uncertainty in her voice. "No one has ever wanted me the way you do. I like it. Especially the way you take control but seem to lose it at the same time."

Jake hissed in a breath, stilled her hand with his. "I do lose control. It's not something I'm proud of."

"Don't you dare apologize again." She squeezed his dick until he winced. "I love it when you take me hard and fast. It's exhilarating. And I liked feeling you inside me without the barrier, and I especially enjoyed feeling you come. It was a first for me. It's…sensual…intimate. Rather primal. It makes me horny thinking about you leaving part of yourself inside me."

"Fuck, woman." Jake dragged her atop him. "You know how to drive me insane."

❧

Sunny straddled his hips, fitting her wet slit to his steel length. His strength was a turn-on, she just wished he'd stop apologizing for making her feel like a goddess. No one ever worshipped her body the way he did.

Placing her palms over his pecs, she explored the hard planes of his torso, committing as much to memory as possible. In a few days, he'd be gone, and her memories would be all she'd have to get her through the lonely nights of the rest of her life. Maybe she'd get over him, eventually, but she didn't see it happening soon. If it were only the sex, the memory would fade, replaced by the pleasure of another lover—eventually. But it wasn't only the sex. Somewhere along the way, he'd burrowed under her skin, straight into her heart.

"You're a wonderful man, Jake Ingram." She leaned down, placed a kiss over his heart. "Will and Rick are lucky to have a brother like you."

"What makes you say so?" He returned the favor by skimming his hands over her breasts, massaging, awakening.

"Few would do what you're doing. You've put everything on hold to chase down leads, to help Will get his life back on track."

"Would you hate me if I told you I had another reason for coming to New York? One that's as selfish as they come?"

"No. You can't change my mind. You're a generous man. Admit it."

"I won't. You can't make me."

"Maybe I can't make you see yourself as others see you." She rocked her hips, slipping easily along his length. "Tell me what selfish endeavor brought you here."

He dropped his hands to the curve of her waist, guiding her to move against him again and again. "You. I came for you. To see if you were as sexy as I remembered. I thought if I could have you once, I'd get you out of my system."

"How did that work out for you, Counselor?"

"Not worth a shit. I want you all the goddamn time." As if to prove it, he lifted her like she weighed nothing then eased her down onto the tip of his shaft. He held her there, poised to take all of him, until her gaze met his. "Ride me, sweetheart. I need to be inside you. Now." He raised his hips while simultaneously applying pressure to her hips, filling her with the proof of his desire.

Sunny cried out. She'd never get enough of him. Never tire of feeling him inside her. He made her feel whole, like he was a piece of her she hadn't known was missing until he filled the empty space inside her. Looking down into his incredible blue eyes, she poured her heart out to him through her gaze and through their intimate connection. She moved over and above him, raising and lowering herself on his shaft, rocking her pelvis against his on every downstroke until he couldn't take it any longer.

He flipped them, easily placing her on her back, then positioning her for maximum penetration. Legs hooked over his shoulders, he braced himself above her by holding her hands above her head. Nose to nose, he powered into her, filling the room with the sound of damp skin slapping against damp skin, and the sound of lungs desperate for air. The old bed creaked beneath them, but both were too far gone to care who they disturbed.

He thrust and thrust. She reveled in each powerful stroke until the friction ignited a flame that grew into a conflagration. Shards of pain morphed into tightly wound coils of pleasure. Meeting his gaze head-on, Sunny greeted each challenge with one of her own until surrender filled his eyes.

"Fuuuuck!" he cried out as his cock swelled, stretching her impossibly wider. He came with a beautiful grimace and a string of curses. The feel of his hot cum bathing her inner walls was the catalyst for her own orgasm. She closed her eyes against the raw pain of muscles seizing and releasing around the hard shaft buried balls-deep inside her.

Tears streamed from her eyes unchecked as she gave herself over to the glory of the moment. He hadn't just pierced her core; he'd tunneled his way into her heart and taken up permanent residence. The tears were happy tears. Tears of joy. Tears of heartache. She was his, but he'd never be hers. Not in the way she wanted. And oh, how she wanted. Everything. His body. His heart. His forever.

Jake dropped his forehead to hers then placed a tiny kiss to her lips. Out of breath, he nuzzled her ear, discovered the tears. "Fuck, Sunny, sweetheart. I fucking hurt you."

She reclaimed one of her hands to cover his mouth before he uttered yet another unwanted apology. "Don't ruin the moment, Jake. I'm fine. Just a little emotional. You have to admit, that was intense."

A smile broke out beneath her fingers, so she dropped her hand to get a better look. "Intense? I guess that's one word for it."

"What would you call it?" she teased, returning his smile.

"Earth-shattering. I think my toes are numb."

Ross insisted they stay for a hearty breakfast before embarking on the next leg of their journey. Assured Scranton was, at most, a two-hour drive away, and since he hadn't heard from his private investigator, they didn't know exactly where they were going anyway, Jake accepted the old man's generosity. The meal of fresh eggs and bacon sourced from a nearby farm beat anything they could have found along the way, and, as he expected from McClelland, the conversation proved interesting.

Ross refilled their coffee mugs. "What if they aren't in Scranton? What are you going to do then?"

Jake reached for another slice of bacon. "We'll be back at square one. Cecil's hometown is our last lead."

Resuming his seat, the older man picked up the thread. "Have you considered the possibility Cecil and Jessica went to someplace she knew about? Does she have family she could have called upon to shelter them? Or like, Cecil, a property they could take advantage of?"

Jake straightened his spine. "No. I've been focused on Hawthorne. Figured he'd call the shots."

Ross pointed a finger at him. "That right there might be where you went wrong. Jessica Blackwell is a manipulator. Cecil was no saint, but when he got caught in Jessica's web, he changed. He did whatever she wanted, even if it wasn't in the best interest of the gallery."

"How do you mean?" Sunny buttered a slice of toast.

"We had a full slate, booked solid a year in advance when she got her hooks into Cecil. Suddenly, we were cancelling showings and filling those dates with artists she brought in. Some were good, like your brother," he said, nodding toward Jake. "Most were mediocre. The gallery was losing money right and left when I retired."

Jake sipped his coffee, letting their host's words roll around in his mind. They ate in silence for a few minutes then something Will said popped into his head. "Will told me if he gets the paintings back, he's going to have a giant bonfire with them."

McClelland's head jerked up. "Why in the world would he do a thing like that?"

Jake raised a hand to ward off more questions. "Hear me out, okay? He says the paintings are crap. In retrospect, he says they shouldn't be part of his portfolio. They don't represent him as an artist, so he wants them destroyed. He said Jessica convinced him to paint what he called more commercial subjects. He argued with her for a while, but, in the end, he followed along. What artist doesn't want easy money, right?" He didn't wait for an answer. "So, what if my brother wasn't the only artist she scammed? What if she manipulated others the way she did him and Cecil?"

"I'm still reeling at the thought of burning one of your brother's paintings, but I see where you're going with this line of thought." His eyebrows furrowed as he sipped at his coffee. "Give me a few minutes to think and I can probably come up with some names for you—artists Jessica brought to Cecil before I left. Maybe the new girl, MacKenzie, could add a few more. I'm not sure what kind of scam Jessica could have been running, but I know she is capable of running one."

Jake wiped his mouth with a paper napkin then stood to take his plate to the sink. "We still need to check out Cecil's home in Scranton, but you may be on to something. I'll let my PI know we want to look in another direction. If you can get me a name, anything to go on, I'd appreciate it."

Ross stood, scraped the scraps from his plate into the trash bin, then placed the plate in the sink. "You two go on, get your stuff together and I'll do the dishes. Nothing like menial chores for thinking. I'll get you a name or two. I promise."

"Thanks." Jake clapped him on the shoulder. "No matter what happens, I owe you. You've been more than generous with your time. And thanks for sharing your art collection with us. I'm glad two of Will's paintings found such a wonderful home."

"Jake's right. We can't thank you enough, on multiple levels." She hugged the old man. "I'd like to stay in touch. Maybe I can rent a car, drive out occasionally to see you?"

"I'd like that. I love it here. Moving was the right thing to do, but sometimes, I miss the art world."

"Anytime you want to talk art, or anything else, call me, okay?"

"Deal." Ross squirted dish soap in the sink. "Now, go on. I know you're eager to get on the road, and I've got some thinking to do."

❧❧

They were halfway to Scranton when Jake's cell phone rang. Seeing Ross's name on the caller ID, he pressed the accept call button on the steering wheel, allowing the call to play through the Jeep's speaker system.

"Hey, Jake, it's me, Ross McClelland. Sorry to bother you, but I've got some names for you."

"You could never be a bother," Sunny said. "We've got you on speaker. Give me a second to get something to write on." She grabbed her purse from the floorboard.

"You guys make it to Scranton yet?"

While Sunny searched for pen and paper, Jake answered, "Not hardly. We ran into road work in three separate places and stopped at a scenic overlook because Sunny wanted to see the bald eagles."

Ross's laughter filled the cab. "Did you see any eagles? They're easier to spot in the winter when the leaves are off the trees."

"We saw one flying over the river, looking for his next meal. It was awesome. They're beautiful birds."

Sunny rejoined the conversation. "He didn't want to stop, but I insisted. The way he talks about it now you'd think it was his idea." She shot Jake a mischievous smile. "I found something to write on. Go ahead with the names." She jotted them down as he rattled off three possible leads.

"Did you talk to your PI yet?" Ross asked.

Jake pointed to a sign advertising another possible stop for them then picked up the conversation. "No. Why?"

106

"Because I thought of something else. Jessica claimed to be a New Yorker, but I overheard her on the phone one day. She'd slipped into a pure Maine accent. At the time, I chalked it up to something fun, you know, playing around, the way people do with accents. Frank and I used to try out our British accents on each other. It was harmless fun, but I remember thinking the conversation sounded serious. I'm thinking now she might have been talking to a relative or an old friend. You might have your PI check records in Maine."

"I wouldn't know a Maine accent if it bit me," Jake supplied.

"They're distinctive," Sunny added. "Hard to fake."

Jake raised an eyebrow. "And you would know this, how?"

"My dad has tried to mimic every accent on the planet at one time or another. Maine gave him a lot of trouble."

"She's right," Ross said. "Anyway, thought I'd mention it."

"Appreciate it." Jake nodded at the mileage sign showing they were getting closer to their destination. "We'll be in Scranton soon. If you think of anything else, no matter how trivial, call. We're grasping at straws here."

"Will do. You two be careful, now. I'll be in touch."

"What do you think?" Sunny asked after Ross hung up. "Could they be in Maine?"

"Anything is possible." He hit the call button on the steering wheel, directed the onboard computer to place a call to his private investigator. While the connection rang through, he added, "I'll get Philip to check it out."

CHAPTER FOURTEEN

Sunny took one look at the house bearing the address
the PI gave them for Cecil Hawthorne's childhood home and
refused to leave the car. "They aren't here. From the looks of
it, no one has been here for decades."

Jake couldn't argue with her assessment since he agreed
with her. The place looked like a crack house with its graffiti-
embellished plywood-covered windows and door. The
landscaping resembled an urban jungle complete with trash
art. He counted six old tires in the front yard alone. From his
perch, he had a view down an equally neglected ribbon
driveway running the length of the house on one side to
another structure. His best guess, a garage. It looked slightly
less shabby than the house, making him wonder if Cecil used
it for something—like to store stolen paintings.

Leaving the engine running, he grabbed the door handle.
"I'll look around. If you see anyone, anyone at all, dial 9-1-1."
His feet hit the faded asphalt roadway. "Stay in the Jeep and
lock the doors. If there's trouble"—he tossed her the key fob
for the keyless ignition—"get the hell out of here."

"Can't we call the cops? Have them come out here and
look around?"

"We could, but this isn't an emergency, so it might be
days before they could spare a patrolman." The worry lines

marring her beautiful visage coaxed him to add, "The place is abandoned. I'll be okay."

"Famous last words."

He smiled though he shared some of her apprehension. For all he knew, someone was cooking meth in the kitchen— or the garage. He wouldn't know until he looked. Leaning in, he beckoned her to meet him halfway. When they were nose to nose, he placed a gentle kiss on her lips. "Lock the doors."

As he trudged along the driveway, he scanned the immediate area. He didn't believe he was in any actual danger. If someone was dealing drugs or cooking meth on the premises, there'd be some signs of life. Trampled grass, trash that wasn't bleached out from long-term exposure to the sun. Everything about the place screamed abandoned property. Except the almost-shiny lock on the garage door. Accounting for weathering, the padlock was maybe a few months old.

He glanced around at the side of the building, noted a grime-encrusted window no one had bothered to board up. He picked his way through thigh-high weeds, being careful where he placed his foot. The last thing he needed was to step on a rusty nail or god knew what else and end up at the emergency room. Reaching the portal, he pressed his face against the glass, blocking outside light with his cupped hands as shields.

Letting out a pent-up breath, he stepped back and shook his head. Nothing. The place was empty save for some old boxes on shelves, none of which were large enough to hide a canvas the size of the ones he was looking for. The entire trip had been a bust.

Shoulders drooping, he returned to the Jeep. The door locks disengaged as he approached. He climbed into the driver's seat, fastened his seat belt, then shifted the transmission into Drive. Not having any idea where he was going, he pulled away from the curb.

"Well?"

She'd waited until he stopped at the first intersection. He gave her credit for restraint. "Well, what?" He turned left, hoping to find his way out of the unfamiliar neighborhood.

"What was in the garage? Were there signs anyone had been there recently?"

"Nothing other than a fairly new lock on the garage door, but I peeked inside. It's empty. We're back to square one."

"Not completely. We still have the Jessica angle to consider. Maybe your PI can come up with some leads in that direction."

They came to a larger road. Jake made an executive decision and turned right. "I need some coffee and we better get gas. Keep your eyes peeled for anything that fits the bill."

Sunny fiddled with her phone. "There's a Dunkin's two miles from here." She pointed out where he should turn. "And where there's a Dunkin's, there's civilization. We should be able to find a gas station nearby."

Jake applauded her navigation skills as she guided him to the promised coffee and donuts across the street from a gas station. "Coffee first." He parked, and they got out and sauntered inside. Taking their steaming cups, they sat at a booth by the window overlooking the parking lot. Jake took a sip, savored the first jolt of caffeine. He rubbed his eyes. "Man, I needed this. Is it me, or does it seem like we ate breakfast a week ago?"

Sunny laughed. "No. I feel the same way. A lot has happened since we ate breakfast with Ross McClelland this morning."

Jake took another sip of the high-octane brew. He didn't realize how much hope he'd assigned to McClelland's lead until he'd looked in the Shupp's garage and saw nothing. The hopelessness of his investigation felt like a load of bricks weighing on his shoulders.

"I'm sorry, Jake." She blew across the top of her cup then took a sip. "I know you were counting on finding the paintings here."

He shrugged. "It's one in a long string of dead ends. I'll get over it." More than anything, he'd wanted to call his brother today with good news.

A church bus pulled up by the front door. A dozen or more kids of varying ages, wearing light-blue T-shirts bearing a summer camp logo, piled out of the conveyance and into the store. Jake's phone vibrated in his pocket. He glanced at the screen. Will. He stood. "I've got to take this." He found a place next to the building where he could hear and speak freely and monitor Sunny through the window.

"Will. What's up?"

"Where are you?"

"Scranton. Why?"

"I got a call from NYPD. One of my paintings turned up at Sotheby's."

"They're sure it's one of the stolen ones?"

"Positive. I have a code I write on the back of every canvas for authentication. I gave them a list of the ones those bastards took. It's definitely one of them."

"Someone waltzed into Sotheby's and consigned it for auction?" Every auction house in the country had been alerted to the theft and instructed to contact NYPD if any of Will's paintings were brought in. Looks like the move paid off.

"Yeah." He could practically see his brother rubbing the back of his neck to ease the tension. "It was a woman. Gave her name and contact info. Turns out she's legit. Has a sales receipt and everything."

"From where?"

"You won't believe it."

"Try me."

"She bought it from Sunnyside Gallery."

Jake's blood ran cold. He glanced at the woman he'd spent the last few days with. Sunny sipped her coffee like she didn't have a care in the world. Anger spiked. He turned, walked to the end of the building where there'd be no chance of being overheard. "When? Who signed the receipt?"

"It's dated two months ago. The receipt is signed by Sunny Sheldon. They questioned the woman who bought the painting. The description she gave of the person who sold it to her matches Sunny to a T. The detective who called me said they were working on search warrants for the gallery and her house."

"Did he leave a number where you could reach him?"

"Yeah. Why?"

"Call him back. Tell him Sunny will be home in three hours."

"How—"

Jake ended the call then turned the device off. No doubt Will would try to call him back to demand an explanation, and he didn't have one to give. Admitting he'd been taken in by a devious woman wasn't high on his list of confessions to make. He'd tell the police everything, let them sort it out. Then he'd go home and figure out how to tell his brother what he'd done.

Leaning against the building, Jake took a few minutes to compose himself. He'd have to continue the charade all the way back to Manhattan. Make small talk. Pretend he wasn't hauling her ass home so the police could question her. Pretend his heart hadn't taken a near-fatal blow.

"Just goes to show, you never really know a person," he mumbled to himself as he opened the door. He held it while the rowdy campers, amped up on sugar, streamed out to their bus.

Pasting a smile on his face, he approached the table where Sunny sat. He picked up his now-cold cup, tossed it in the nearest trash. "You ready? We need to get back to the city."

Sunny stood, tossed her cup in the receptacle. He gassed up across the street then they hit the freeway. If they didn't run across construction delays or major traffic getting into the city, he'd have Sunny home within the time frame he'd given his brother.

❧❦

"Who was that on the phone?" Sunny waited until Jake navigated the complex streets to get to the freeway to question the tension she'd sensed in him since he'd returned from taking the call.

"Work. I need to go home sooner than I'd planned."

Sunny nodded. "Okay." She turned her attention to the road. He wasn't in the mood to talk. She understood, or thought she did. She didn't know much about his life in Texas, but she sort of understood lawyers. If a client needed him, he'd have to go. "If your PI comes up with anything on Jessica, let me know. I can follow up if you need me to."

"No need. If he finds something, I'll have him do the legwork. I wouldn't want to put you in danger."

She didn't know what changed, but something sure had. This wasn't the Jake Ingram she knew. That man was warm and funny and didn't snap a person's head off for offering to help. She snapped back. "I'm not stupid. I wouldn't put myself in danger, but I can drive by an address or… I don't know…something."

"No need for you to be involved. You've done enough."

"What do you mean I've done enough?" She couldn't keep the scorn out of her voice.

"It means, you've done plenty. This is a wild-goose chase. Will doesn't even want the paintings back. I've wasted too much time already on this. I've got to get home. I have other clients who need my attention."

Something was wrong, but she had no clue what it could be. And Jake wasn't talking. She'd been a fool to think there could be anything between them other than passionate sex. She'd miss the sex, no doubt about it, but as the miles sped by, her heart told her she'd miss the man even more. She already missed him. The person who'd left the donut shop to take a phone call wasn't the same one who'd walked back in. "That must have been some phone call," she muttered.

"You don't know the half of it."

"Are we going to have lunch? Or do I need to crawl over the seat and get the cooler we stocked? I'm hungry."

"There's got to be a drive-thru out here somewhere. We'll get something to eat on the road."

A half hour later, they picked up sandwiches and sodas at a fast-food chain then got right back on the highway. They'd left Pennsylvania behind and were well into New Jersey when he spoke to her again. "I'll drop you at your house then I'm going to the airport. See if I can catch a flight this afternoon."

She reached for her phone. "I can book you a flight."

"Don't bother. I have a return ticket, so it's just a matter of changing it."

She put her phone away. "Okay. I was only trying to help."

"I don't need your help. I can manage on my own."

Sunny bit her bottom lip to keep from saying something she'd regret later. When he took the Lincoln Tunnel instead of the George Washington Bridge, she kept her mouth shut. Let him slog through midtown traffic to get uptown. He didn't want her help. She wouldn't give it.

A stalled car in the tunnel and the usual heavy afternoon Manhattan traffic added almost an hour to what would have been a simple drive from the bridge to her brownstone. Sunny inwardly snickered at the typical tourist mistake. If the obstinate man couldn't admit he needed help, then who was she to offer it? It was his car, his gas, his time. She'd already decided the summer was too hot to stay in the city. She'd do some laundry then pack up and go to her dad's beach house for a week or two. Let Ginger run the gallery. Maybe she'd drag her painting supplies out of storage and take them with her. Talking with Ross McClelland opened her eyes to her discontent. Helping artists find homes for their work was satisfying, but deep down, she wanted to create. She'd let doubts about her talent get in her way.

No one was stopping her now. Even if her work stank up the entire Hamptons, she didn't care. She'd take the emotions crowding her chest, making her eyes water with tears she refused to shed, and pour them all onto canvas.

What did it matter if it came out a colossal mess? And if painting wasn't enough of an outlet, there were plenty of outdoor activities like running, biking, and swimming she could indulge in to help get Jake Ingram out of her system. In a few weeks, she'd be good as new. Ready to come back to the city and her solitary life.

The atmosphere in the car grew colder with each block. By the time Jake turned down her street, she wouldn't have been surprised to find icicles hanging off his nose. When she glanced his way, the hard set of his jaw and the white-knuckle grip he had on the steering wheel spoke volumes. He'd shut her out completely.

She pointed out her house. "No need to hunt a parking spot. I'll grab my bag, and you can get on with whatever's turned you into a man I don't know." She opened the door, dropped to the street. Before she slammed the back hatch down, she volleyed her parting shot. "Have a nice life, Jake Ingram."

She'd muscled her suitcase inside and shut the door when her doorbell rang. Figuring she must have left something, and Jake brought it, she didn't bother looking through the peephole. She gasped at the man standing there, his NYPD gold shield held up for her inspection. "Are you Sunny Sheldon?"

"Yes. What's this about?"

He produced a folded sheet of paper from his jacket pocket. "I'm Detective Antonio Reeves, NYPD, and this is a warrant to search the premises." He slapped the document into her hand then brushed past her. Before she could catch her breath, four uniformed officers and a woman in plain-clothes followed him inside.

The female detective ushered Sunny over to the sofa and insisted she have a seat. She needn't have. It was all Sunny could do to take the few steps without her knees buckling.

"I don't understand." She could hear drawers opening and closing upstairs, and someone was in the kitchen from the sound of the cabinet doors slamming. "What's this about?"

"It's all in the warrant. You can contact your lawyer. In fact, I'd advise you to do so sooner rather than later."

It took a moment for the woman's words to register. "Am I under arrest?"

"Not yet. But you will need to answer some questions. You can answer them here or down at the station."

"But I haven't done anything."

"That's what they all say."

Hands shaking, Sunny unfolded the document. One line stood out—suspected of the possession and sale of stolen goods."

She looked up. "I've never stolen a thing in my life!"

"We believe otherwise, thus the warrant."

"But…" She couldn't think of anything else to say. The fog cleared. She took a longer look at the official document, looking for something to explain what they were doing to her house. What she found turned her blood to ice and went a long way to explaining Jake's sudden shift from friend to cold enemy. But it still didn't explain why? Why her? She'd cooperated with the police, and she'd spent the last few days helping Jake chase down leads.

When she'd read the entire thing, she pulled her phone from her pocket. Her dad answered on the second ring.

"Sunny! To what do I owe this pleasure?"

"You can thank the NYPD, Dad. I need a lawyer. Can you get me one?"

The conversation became stilted. She didn't want to say anything in front of the detective he could misconstrue, so she kept her comments to a minimum while still trying to convey to her father what kind of mess she was in. "I'm sorry, Dad," she said, winding down. "The media will have a field day with this."

"I'll call my lawyer, get him over to your place ASAP then I'll call my publicist and sick him on the story. He'll get out ahead of this thing. This is all an enormous mistake, Sunshine. Don't you worry about a thing."

Talking to her dad helped, but once the lead detective finished tearing her house apart and came to sit on the opposite sofa, a wide pit opened in her stomach, threatening to swallow her whole. Shock had long since been replaced by anger. She possessed infinite respect for the NYPD, but they'd gotten this all wrong. "I didn't steal anything from anyone, and I don't know the whereabouts of the paintings you're looking for. I do know they're too big to hide in my kitchen cabinets or any drawer in this house."

Detective Reeves flipped to a fresh page in his notebook. "I'm aware of the size of the paintings. I have photos of them, but you never know what you'll find in someone's house."

"What's that supposed to mean?"

"It means, would you like to explain why three of the paintings you claim you don't know the whereabouts of are in your basement?"

"What?" Sunny's heart felt like it would pound right out of her chest. "That's not possible."

"Can you explain this sales receipt from your gallery for one of the stolen paintings?" He held up a photocopy of a receipt bearing the Sunnyside Gallery logo. It looked legitimate, but she was quickly learning looks could be deceiving.

"It has to be a forgery. I'm not a thief, and even if I was, I wouldn't be stupid enough to sell stolen paintings out of my gallery."

"Yet, that's exactly what happened."

The detective stood. Reflexively, Sunny followed suit. "Sunny Sheldon, you're under arrest for possession of stolen goods and for the sale of stolen property."

CHAPTER FIFTEEN

Jake took the phone call minutes before boarding his flight from JFK to Dallas. "You found some of the paintings in her home?"

"Three, to be exact. She maintains she didn't know they were there and claims no knowledge of the rest. As soon as we book her, I'll serve the search warrant on the gallery."

"I don't mean to sound like I don't trust you, but you're certain they're originals?"

"I'm no expert, but they match the photographs your brother provided, and the inventory codes on the back match up."

Jake pinched the bridge of his nose. He'd developed a headache shortly after receiving Will's phone call, and it had only gotten worse with time. He looked forward to several hours in first class and a couple of stiff drinks. "I appreciate all you've done, Detective, and Will sends his thanks for all your hard work. I'm about to get on a plane, but please, call or text me with any updates to the situation."

He sat, elbows on his knees, his hands clasped, head bowed, trying to reconcile the woman he knew with the one he now suspected her of being. The ache in his chest was real. Probably the only genuine thing to come out of these last few days. He'd fallen in love with a woman only to find out she wasn't who he thought she was. As a lawyer, he understood people lied—all the time—and he'd developed a radar for deceit. Not once did Sunny set his radar off.

He didn't know what the oversight said about him, but he vowed never to let anyone snooker him the way she had. If they found Will's paintings at her gallery, what kind of idiot would he be? He'd been there a few days ago and never thought to look around. He'd blindly taken everyone's word regarding Sunny's character.

Jake waited until the last call before boarding. Seated in the plush first-class seat, drink in hand, he closed his eyes and painstakingly relived every minute he'd spent with the woman, from the time she noticed him standing on the sidewalk outside her gallery until she sat across from him in the Scranton donut shop. Several drinks and thousands of painful memories later, he still couldn't find any link between Sunny, the self-aware pseudo-celebrity/businessperson he'd fallen for and the heartless criminal she now appeared to be.

Yet, the evidence was there. Will's paintings were in her home. The detective forwarded him a copy of the gallery receipt as well. Nothing about it looked fake. Which only proved she was more of an actor than anyone gave her credit for. What did they say about being a chip off the old block?

Waving the flight attendant down, he ordered another drink and downed it in one gulp. He'd surpassed his self-imposed limit long ago, but if there was ever a day to self-medicate with alcohol, this was it. Back in Scranton, when he'd leaned into the Jeep to remind her to lock the doors, he'd been on the verge of telling her he loved her. Just in case something happened to him, since he hadn't known if the place was empty or a paranoid neighbor would shoot first and ask questions later.

"Bad day?" the lady in the window seat next to him asked.

He wasn't in the mood to talk. He grunted out, "I've had better," then closed his eyes, hoping to discourage anymore conversation. His attitude worked because she left him alone the rest of the flight.

Will and Rick waited for him at the baggage carousel. Rick had his own fledgling home remodeling business, and their middle brother helped him when he could. They'd both hopped in the car without bothering to change out of their work clothes. He hugged them anyway.

"Have you looked at your phone lately?" Will asked as he and Jake trailed Rick across several lanes of traffic to the parking garage.

"No. I turned it off for the flight."

"You probably have a dozen messages from Detective Reeves."

He was still feeling the effects of over imbibing, not to mention he'd be happy if he never heard a certain woman's name again for the rest of his life. "I gather you've been talking to him, so why don't you fill me in?"

They'd driven his car to the airport. Will had yet to purchase wheels, and Rick's old construction truck sounded like it was on its last legs. Even if he would need to have the interior detailed after they sat their dirty asses in it, he was grateful they'd both shown up for him. He let Rick play chauffeur, while Will rode shotgun. Once they'd navigated off the airport grounds, Will filled him in on what he'd missed over the last few hours.

"Reeves called a while ago. They arrested Sunny Sheldon."

"Yeah, that happened before I boarded."

"The rest of my paintings were in a storage room at her gallery. All but the one she sold."

Jake pinched his temples between his thumb and forefinger. "Shit."

"She claims she's innocent." Will's voice remained flat, noncommittal.

He glared at the back of Will's head. "All evidence to the contrary."

"As you say."

They drove straight into the setting sun. Jake didn't

know which was worse, the harsh light driving nails into his skull or the way the world spun when he closed his eyes, waiting for his brother to drop the next bomb on his head.

"She also said she spent the last few days driving around upstate with you."

He hadn't planned on telling anyone about the time he'd spent with Sunny, but that ship had sailed, and apparently sunk, thank you, NYPD. As if Jake wasn't already the biggest ass this side of the Mississippi, Will verbally kicked him one more time. "I take it she didn't lie about her whereabouts?"

"Fuck off." If anyone deserved an explanation, it was his brother. But he couldn't think of anything to say that wouldn't make him look like an incompetent jerk who let the wrong head do his thinking.

As if he'd heard Jake's thoughts, Will said, "You don't owe me an explanation, but Detective Reeves is going to want one."

"Fuck." The last thing he wanted to do was explain why he'd spent the better part of a week, traveling with and screwing a prime suspect in the theft of his brother's art. Especially when he'd been acting as Will's attorney. It didn't sound any better in his mind than it would to Detective Reeves's ears. He'd fucked, literally, with the investigation. Convincing the detective he hadn't known would be the trick.

Will shifted in his seat, graced Jake with a smile. "Don't sweat it, Bro. None of us suspected Sunny, and she's a beautiful woman. If she'd looked at me the way she looked at my paintings, I would have tried harder to get her into my bed." His brows furrowed. "Never would have suspected her." He swung around, leaving Jake with the vision of his brother flirting with Sunny.

The image shouldn't have affected him. It wasn't the first time the brothers had been attracted to the same woman. They were too close in age not to have friends in common. Over the years, they'd each lost a conquest to one or the other brother, but thinking about Sunny with Will made him want to beat his brother to a pulp. Sunny was his. For a few days. Nothing more. She'd betrayed Will then used Jake to deflect the investigation as far away from her as possible. Whatever feelings he'd developed for her were dead. Had to be.

The media storm hit the next day in New York. Interest in the crime dwindled quickly when it went unsolved for so many months. Now that a minor celebrity had been arrested and brought up on charges, it was headline news again. Everyone was looking for an angle.

Will wasn't answering his phone. He sent every call to voicemail where a recording declared he had no comment. It was only a matter of time before Jake's name became part of the narrative.

"You need to get yourself a new lawyer," he informed his brother that evening. "I've already talked to Randy. He's willing to take you on as a client." Randy Wallace was the other attorney in town. He was closer to Will's age than Jake's, and they shared a close friendship with another local, Hank Travis, who'd made it big as a rock star. Randy handled all of Hank's legal needs and was probably better equipped to deal with the media frenzy headed Will's way. Jake was considering hiring him to handle with the shitstorm he'd created for himself.

Will paced Jake's office. "Do we have to drag Randy into this? Why can't you handle it?" He stopped, and, hands on his hips, he faced Jake. "I'm the victim here. I don't see why I should need a lawyer, but since I do, I'd prefer you."

Jake stared his brother down. "You need someone to protect your rights and your reputation. Not every reporter or blogger or whatever has scruples. Some of them make shit up rather than admit they know nothing."

"I get it, but I still want you to handle it. Not that I don't trust Randy, I do. He'd never screw me over, but you're family."

"All the more reason to hire someone else. Anything I dispute will look suspicious because we're related. And have you forgotten? I've got my own storm brewing on the horizon. It's only a matter of time before some reporter finds out I was screwing a witness all over upstate New York, and it was me who returned her to her home the day they arrested her." He rocked back in his chair. "I'm considering retaining Randy myself."

"Go right ahead," Will said. "I think you should, but I'll stick with you."

"Why?"

His brother flashed him a shit-eating smile. "Because I'd have to pay Randy."

Jake sat forward, propped his elbows on his desk, and dropped his head into his upturned hands. "Fuck you."

Will sank into one of the ancient visitor's chairs. All humor leached from his voice. "Seriously, man. I know you have your own troubles, and if you need Randy in your corner, I'll pay for his services, but there's no reason my shit has to fall on you. I've already asked MacKenzie to draft a press release for me. I'll make a public statement, say what I want to say, and tell them to leave me the fuck alone."

Jake raised his head. Will sat sprawled out like he hadn't a care in the world. It was all an act. He knew his brother well. Of the three of them, he was the best at hiding his feelings. That was why when Will came home from New York, broke and broken, Jake jumped in to do whatever he could. Getting the funds restored to Will's bank accounts helped his brother move on, but Will did the real work himself through self-reflection and painting. Art had always been Will's outlet of choice, and he did it better than anyone Jake had ever known. He wished he had something as productive to help him deal with the guilt and failure he felt in relation to Will's case.

"The press release is a good idea," he conceded. "Probably won't shut them up for long, but it might buy you a few weeks."

"That's all I need. You know how it is. Something else will happen, and the media will drop my story faster than you can say polish my dick. I'll drop from front-page news to the back page of the Sunday Arts section overnight."

"I hope you're right." He hoped some celebrity would do something stupid today or tomorrow. Anything to deflect attention from their story.

"You know I am. That's the way the media works." Will pushed to his feet. "Are we good? You hire Randy if you think you need the distance, but you're still my attorney?"

Jake stood, rounded the desk, and grabbed his brother in a bear hug. None of that bro hug shit between blood brothers. He clapped Will on the back. "I'm still your attorney, but I'm sending you a big, fat bill when this is over."

Will shoved him in the shoulder. "You bill me, asshole, and I'll tell everyone about the half-done manuscripts you keep hidden under your bed."

His brother was driving away before Jake recovered enough to make his feet move. Standing in the doorway watching Will take off in Rick's old truck, Jake shook his head. He should have known. There wasn't anything sacred between brothers.

"Shit." He slammed the door then turned to see Jean, his secretary/paralegal, smiling at him.

"Family," she said. "Can't live with them. Can't kill them."

❧❧

Jake spent the better part of an hour that afternoon on a video chat with Detective Reeves and his partner, a female detective he'd met on the sidewalk outside Sunny's brownstone. It was a typical good cop, bad cop interview designed to scare the truth out of a suspect. Only Jake wasn't a suspect, and no cop was going to intimidate him into revealing anything he didn't want to.

He told his story, concisely, leaving out intimate details that weren't anybody's business but his and Sunny's. No matter what she'd done, they were consenting adults.

"We appreciate your time, Mr. Ingram," Detective

Reeves wound up the questioning.

"I wish I could help you, but she gave no indication she knew anything about the paintings. Just the opposite, in fact."

"She's still maintaining her innocence. Says she doesn't have a clue how they got in the basement of her home or in the storeroom at her gallery. She's convincing."

"I guess the acting genes run in the family after all," he said.

"We'll see. She's agreed to a lie detector test."

"Let me know how the test turns out."

"Sure thing. Oh, and you can tell your brother we'll ship the recovered paintings to him in a week or two. We're getting an art expert to authenticate them for the record first. The DA assures us photos and the documentation from the expert will be enough in court."

"I'll tell Will to be on the lookout for them. Speaking of being on the lookout… Any sign of Cecil Hawthorne and Jessica Blackwell?"

"None. Ms. Sheldon swears she barely knows them and has no idea where they went."

Jake recalled the conversation he'd had with Sunny right before he'd taken Will's call. "I have another thought. We'd reached a brick wall trying to track down Hawthorne. Then it hit me. Maybe we should take a harder look at Jessica Blackwell. We've been under the assumption Cecil was calling the shots, but what if it was Jessica? When we were talking to Ross McClelland, he mentioned overhearing her on the phone one day, and she'd slipped into an accent he associated with people from Maine. I asked the private investigator I hired to do a little digging."

"McClelland thought the accent was real?"

"He said she claimed to be a New Yorker, but it seemed to him she'd lapsed into the accent without realizing it, which suggests it might be something she's worked to get rid of."

"Ever tried to get rid of your Texas twang, Mr. Ingram?"

"Once, in law school. My professors at Harvard said I needed to lose it if I wanted to be successful outside my home state. After a few weeks working with a Ph.D. candidate from the speech lab at the university, I gave up. Too much work."

"You're right about one thing. Changing your speech patterns is hard, and there aren't many reasons people go to all the trouble."

"Actors do it all the time. Lots of Aussies and Brits playing American's in films and on TV these days."

"And criminals trying to blend in. A distinct accent makes a person memorable."

"It might be nothing, but I thought I'd mention it."

"If you think of anything else, or if your PI comes up with a lead, let us know."

They ended the call not exactly as a team, but Jake felt like he was no longer under the microscope. He called Will, filled him in on the conversation. "I came clean. Told the detectives I'd literally fucked up and apologized for any harm my actions might have done to the investigation."

"You couldn't have known, Jake. Forget about it."

"I'll try." He didn't think he'd ever forget the way Sunny felt in his arms, moving beneath him, on top of him. For a few days, he'd known the magic of being with the right person. Only Sunny wasn't the right person. Her betrayal cut deep, and he wasn't sure the wound to his heart would ever heal. Shaking off those thoughts, he related what the detective said about Will's paintings.

"I need to have a bonfire. I was thinking down by the lake at your house."

"Works for me. I've been wanting to build a firepit close to the shoreline. Maybe we can work on it together?"

"Sure thing. I'll see if Rick wants to help. You pick out the stone, and I'll pay. It's the least I can do since I'm not going to pay you for your actual work."

Even though his asshole brother couldn't see him over the phone, Jake shook his head. "I should have drowned you when you were a baby."

"Nah. You love me; you just won't admit it."

Damn straight. He loved both his brothers. "If you say so." He hung up without saying goodbye. As predicted, a text came through within seconds. Jake opened it, laughed at the obscene emoji, and fired one back. "Asshole," he muttered before muting his phone and getting back to work.

CHAPTER SIXTEEN

Jake handed Will another brick then returned to the pallet that had been delivered earlier in the week. Because all three brothers were swamped with work, they'd put off building Jake's new fire pit until the weekend. It was the first time they'd been together in ages and longer since they'd worked on anything together.

"Last time we built something had to be the treehouse," he mused out loud. "Remember that?"

Rick chuckled. "By treehouse, you mean a couple of rotted boards nailed into the fork of that old oak behind the house." He held his hand out for another brick. "I think the rusty nails are still there but the wood disintegrated years ago."

Rick would know, he still lived in the house they'd grown up in and the oak he spoke of still shaded most of the backyard. "It was more than a few boards, and they weren't rotten when we put them up there."

Will tossed a pebble at Jake's head. "You know what they say, your memory is the first thing to go."

Jake picked up the pebble and tossed it, hitting Will square in the back. "Eyesight, asshole. Your eyesight is the first thing to go." God, he missed hanging out with his brothers.

"We need to do this more often," he said, unloading an armload of bricks where either brother could reach them.

"Fuck off," Rick said, adding another row to the rapidly growing ring. "You just want the free labor."

"Not true. Besides, I'm paying you with food and all the beer you can drink." With the toe of his boot, he nudged a brick closer to Will.

His middle brother sat back on his heels and used his T-shirt to wipe sweat from his brow. "Tell me again why you didn't hire someone to build this thing?"

"Because you said you'd do it, asswipe. As I recall, our verbal contract included your labor in lieu of my billable hours on your behalf."

Rick grabbed a water bottle he kept nearby, took a drink, then poured the rest over his head. "I didn't agree to do anything, so why am I here?"

Will threw a clod of dirt at the youngest Ingram brother. "You're here because you're too stupid to say no."

"Hey!" Rick used his forearm to shield his eyes from the missile. "Who gave you a job when you came home with your tail tucked between your legs?" He launched his own attack, hitting Will square in the chest with a lump of soil.

"Fuck you!"

Jake snagged himself another beer from the cooler then dropped into the folding lawn chair he'd brought to the build site earlier and watched his younger brothers have at each other. "Just like old times," he mumbled to himself then took a long pull from the bottle.

The two of them tussled like idiots since they were kids. When they were little, it usually ended when one of them got hurt. It had been years since he'd seen either of them smile the way they were, so he figured he'd let it go on for a while longer before he broke it up.

They were winding down when a distinctly female voice cut through the heat like a sharp knife. "William Ingram! Stop that. Right now!"

All three brothers turned toward the source and froze.

MacKenzie Carlysle stopped behind Jake's chair, a frown marring her beautiful face. Will was the first to recover. He shoved Rick off him and stood, dusting his clothes off as he approached the woman he'd fallen for. "Kenzie! What brings you out here?"

She held up a hand to keep him from getting too close. "I came out to check on the project." Her gaze cut from Will to Rick to Jake then back to Will. "Looks like I arrived in the nick of time. What were you two fighting about?"

"I don't know." Will glanced at Rick. "You remember?"

Rick stood, used the hem of his T-shirt to clean his face. "Nope."

Jake opened the lid of the cooler sitting next to his chair, a silent invitation for everyone to have something cool to drink. "They used to tussle all the time when they were kids. Drove Mom nuts."

Kenzie pulled a soda from the ice, popped the top. "And you didn't stop them?"

"Why would I? Seeing them get in trouble was one of the few perks of being the oldest."

Rick limped over, helped himself to another water bottle. "I don't remember hurting this bad when we were kids."

Will smiled. "Me, either." He rubbed the small of his back. "No fair using your military training."

"Like grinding a fistful of dirt in my face was fair? Asshole. You're lucky I didn't fuck you up for real."

MacKenzie huffed and stomped her foot on the hardpacked lawn. She glared at Will. "Really? You shoved dirt in your brother's face?"

"Hey, you should have seen what he did to me."

It was time to step in. Jake kicked out at Will then Rick, missing both with his big boots. "Enough. Playtime is over. If Mom were here, she'd make you kiss and make up, but I'll settle for a handshake."

The brother's complied then they both sat to finish their drinks. Jake stood, offering Mac the only seat in the house for the construction show. She declined, choosing to sit on the grass a safe distance from her smelly boyfriend.

"The fire pit looks like it's coming along," she said.

"A couple more hours then we'll be done, except for hauling the landscape rock over"—Jake pointed to the pile of stones next to the pallet of bricks—"and spreading it out."

"You can do that yourself," Rick complained.

"Got some day laborers coming tomorrow to finish up," Jake admitted. "They'll put in a path from the pool deck, too. Make it easier to get to the lake from the house."

"Then we need to finish this." Will climbed to his feet. He kicked Rick's foot. "Come on, jerk wad. I want to have time for a dip in the pool while Jake grills the steaks, so let's get busy."

"Okay, okay." Rick rolled to his hands and knees then boosted himself up. "You'd think I'd be in better shape," he groused as he followed Will back to the work site where a fire pit was slowly taking shape.

"I'm surprised they've gotten as much done as they have," MacKenzie remarked.

"They've been working hard. They were having fun. I didn't have the heart to make them stop."

"Did Will tell you the paintings are on the way? They're supposed to arrive on Tuesday. He had them shipped to your house."

Jake finished his beer. "No. He didn't mention it, but that's okay."

"You think he'll really burn them?"

"Yep. I do."

"Aren't you going to talk him out of it?"

He reached for a water bottle, twisted the cap off, and downed half the bottle. He stood. "They're his. If he says they're crap, then I'll take his word for it." He walked to the pile of bricks, grabbed another armload. Thinking about Will's paintings brought things better forgotten to mind.

It had been weeks since he'd heard from his PI or the detectives in charge of Will's case. The last phone call from Detective Reeves was to let him know Sunny made bail and passed the polygraph test. The tests were so unreliable they weren't allowed in court, so passing one meant nothing. Especially for someone with acting in their blood. Sunny was wasting her talent, Jake decided. He considered himself an excellent judge of character, but she'd reeled him in, hook, line, and sinker. His heart still ached where her barbs had sunk into the vulnerable muscle. At night, he lay awake, the memory of their numerous bouts of sex taking possession of his body. At the time, he'd been sure the sex had been more, but now he refused to believe it was anything more than a physical release for both of them.

The following Saturday, the brothers gathered around the firepit. Will invited some witnesses—MacKenzie and an old friend of the Ingram brother's, Hank Travis and his wife, Melody. He handed Jake his cell phone. "I want this on video. Every step. I don't want anyone to question what happened to these paintings. No chance copies can be passed off as the originals."

Following Will's instructions, Jake documented the removal of each canvas from the stack, getting a clear shot of the coding on the back and the actual painting before the artist himself, then added it to the firepit. By the time he'd added the last one to the pit, the pyramid was shoulder high and multiple canvases deep.

Before he lit the kindling they'd placed around the base of the structure, Will stood in front of the camera. "I, W.H. Ingram, solemnly swear the paintings you see here are the originals, and, to my knowledge, no copies exist. These paintings never represented who I was as an artist at the time I painted them, and they don't represent who I am now. Call me temperamental or insane, I don't care. They're mine, and I'll do with them as I please. This is what I please."

He touched a propane lighter to the lighter fluid-soaked kindling. Flames shot up, catching the oil paints on the nearest canvas. Within seconds, the entire pyramid erupted.

Will stepped back. Jake put a hand on one of his shoulders, and Rick did the same on the other, offering their support, a wall of solidarity. The three of them, along with the witnesses, watched as the fire consumed over a year's worth of Will's work. No one spoke until nothing but ashes remained.

Will stepped in front of the camera. "This has not been a hoax. Everything you saw was real. The following witnesses are here to attest to the authenticity of the event." He named each one in attendance as Jake slowly panned to include the solemn group in the video document. When he'd completed the task, he turned the camera on himself and added his statement of authenticity for the record before ending the recording.

Jake stepped forward. "At Will's request, there's champagne poolside. Shall we go toast to my brother's future?" His statement broke everyone out of the trance they'd been in. Suddenly, everyone was talking at once as they made their way along the new stone pathway to the expansive pool deck where buckets held bottles of bubbly on ice.

Corks flew. Glasses bubbled over with the golden liquid as they toasted to Will's new direction in life. Inside Jake's house, easels bore several paintings bearing the signature of William H. Ingram—proof the artist had moved on from the crime that nearly destroyed him.

Jake found Will staring at a nude he'd done of MacKenzie. As stunning as her body was, strategically draped with a swath of white fabric, it was the emotion in her eyes, the hint of a smile on her lips that truly caught Jake's attention. He'd once thought he'd seen the same expression on Sunny's face after he'd made love to her, but he'd been wrong. He hoped Will wasn't seeing what he wanted to see instead of what was actually there. He rested a hand on his brother's shoulder. "You okay?"

"Yeah. I thought it would be harder to let them go. I don't think I realized how far I've come since all this happened until they went up in flames. It was like a giant weight lifted off my shoulders. A fresh start."

"I spent some time looking at them this week."

Will cut his gaze to Jake. "You did?"

Jake shrugged. "They were in my garage. Figured you wouldn't mind too much if I checked them out."

"No. I don't mind. What did you think?"

"I'm not an art critic, but having seen your earlier work, and now, seeing your more recent paintings, I have to agree with you. They were good, but they weren't you. I don't know how to explain it, but they lacked something…"

"Heart. Soul," his brother supplied.

"Yeah, I think you summed it up." They stared at the painting of MacKenzie for a few minutes. "This is extraordinary. You poured your heart into it."

"I did. I'm in love with her, Jake."

"She loves you?"

"What do you think?" He nodded at the canvas. "Or did I fail to convey her emotions?"

"No, you nailed it, Bro. Just hoping you aren't imagining things."

"You sound like you're doubting yourself. You think Sunny lied to you?"

Jake ground his molars and rocked back on his heels. He hadn't gone into detail about the time he'd spent with Sunny in New York, but Will seemed to have come to some very accurate conclusions all on his own. He'd always possessed a knack for reading Jake's mind and his moods. It could be damn irritating sometimes. Like now. Jake drew a deep breath, let it out. "I know she lied to me. She's had your paintings all along."

"I don't think so." Will faced him. "I'm convinced she didn't have anything to do with the theft." He tapped Jake's chest. "And deep in your heart, you know she didn't."

Maybe, but admitting it would mean he couldn't ignore what had happened between them, and he wasn't ready to go there. Not yet. "I was surprised you invited Hank and Melody to this little burn party." The couple were friends with Sunny. Their connection with the gallery owner brought MacKenzie to Willowbrook.

"You think they knew something?" Will's hostile stance, hands fisted on his hips, called Jake on his inference. "You've known Hank Travis since you were both in diapers. He's a world-famous musician. He's worth millions. You can't really believe he or his wife had anything to do with this."

Jake sipped from the flute he held. God, he hated champagne. He downed the remaining liquid in one gulp, silently vowing to hit the liquor cabinet for a proper drink as soon as possible. Right now, his brother demanded an answer. "No, I don't think Hank had anything to do with stealing your paintings." At his brother's raised eyebrow, he added, "Melody didn't, either." Will made a *come on, you aren't done yet* sign with his hand. Jake shook his head. "I'll take your word when it comes to MacKenzie, but you have to admit, this entire thing looks fishy."

"Damn right it does. I know I won't convince you tonight, but mark my words, Bro, Sunny is innocent. The sooner you get your head out of your ass and admit it, the sooner you'll find the assholes who ripped me off and set her up to take the fall." He poked Jake in the chest then delivered his parting shot. "I hope you yank your head out before you suffocate on your own shit."

He didn't bother to stop Will, though the urge to punch his lights out was strong. The man had a romantic streak a mile wide. It served him well as an artist, but he stuck his nose in other people's business. Like the time he'd tried to set Rick up with a cheerleader. She'd been mildly interested but failed to mention she'd been secretly dating the quarterback at a rival high school for several months. The jock took exception to Rick asking her out. All three brothers ended up in the principal's office over the ensuing fistfight. Jake, quarterback for Willowbrook High, had been forced to sit out an important game, which the home team lost. Will and Rick both served a week in detention.

Perhaps Will had lost his romantic tendencies for a while and ended up in the clutches of Jessica Blackwell and company, but along with his money and the paintings, he'd also recovered his romantic heart.

Just my luck.

Jake took one last look at the painting of MacKenzie. "I hope it's not all an act, Bro," he muttered to himself then stalked off to find something with a lot more kick than champagne.

Sunny tucked her hands into the pockets of the old sweater she'd found in the closet at her dad's South Hampton house then set off along the beach. The summer heat had broken, and the leaves were turning. Most of the neighbors had returned to the city to enjoy the upcoming holidays, leaving the beach deserted—just the way Sunny liked it.

She'd come to her dad's place in the Hamptons the same day they released her on bail with only the clothes on her back and a new appreciation for privacy. Over the past few months, she'd taken to online shopping to curate a wardrobe to replace the one she'd left behind. She'd gotten a glimpse at what the police had done to her home before they arrested her, and she never wanted to touch any of her possessions again. They'd gone through everything from her kitchen cabinets to her most intimate clothes to the box of tampons she kept in the cabinet beneath the bathroom sink.

Her dad's assistant coordinated the cleanup efforts. With her dad's help, he'd boxed up her photos and other personal mementos. Those went into storage. They'd tossed or donated everything else to local charities, including all her clothing and furniture. She'd rented the brownstone out to a couple with two small children. When this was over, she'd find another place to live. Maybe a chicken farm upstate.

A brisk wind lifted her overlong hair, swirled it around her face. She stopped, looked out to sea as she attempted to tame the wayward strands. The gray sky matched her mood. Not a good sign. She'd spent enough time on the tip of Long Island to know storms could brew up in a matter of minutes and wreak havoc almost without warning. Like life, she mused, drawing the fresh, salty air into her lungs. Unlike the storm making its way ashore now, she hadn't seen the one coming that destroyed her career and her life. One minute she was sipping coffee, wondering if she'd like living in Texas because Jake would be miserable in New York—and the next, she'd been in handcuffs, facing a judge and pleading not guilty to a slew of charges she still couldn't wrap her head around.

And the man she'd fallen in love with disappeared. Left her to face the worst days of her life all alone.

She rubbed at the ache lodged deep inside her chest—a raw wound where her heart had once been. Jake's defection hurt more than she'd believed possible. She'd expected him to at least want to hear her side of the story, but he'd passed judgment, even played the role of her own, personal Judas, delivering her home so they could arrest her. It took her a while to put the events leading up to her arrest all together, but once she did, her lawyer confirmed her suspicions. Jake had known about the painting they'd accused her of selling even before she did. That explained his behavior on the ride from Scranton to Manhattan.

If he'd only asked, she could have told him she'd been set up. Somehow. By someone.

Sunny couldn't remember the last time she'd been in the brownstone's basement. Perhaps when the boiler needed repair? That had been last winter. But she visited the gallery storeroom, almost daily. Every item stored there had been meticulously documented, both for inventory and for insurance. Nothing went in or came out without the movement being noted in the logbook she kept in her office. According to her lawyer, the paintings hadn't been entered into the logbook. She'd pointed that out as a plus on her side, but he'd been quick to point out a thief would hardly keep an official record of the stolen items they had on the premises.

The real kicker was, she'd seen the photos the police department's hired art expert had taken of the paintings and knew she never would have consigned them, much less risked everything to steal them. Jake's brother was right. They weren't the quality product W.H. Ingram was capable of.

She'd thought not finding her fingerprints on any of the canvases was another chink in the case, but as her lawyer pointed out, she kept a supply of cotton gloves handy and donned them anytime she handled the artwork in her gallery. The police hadn't been able to explain how she'd broken into Hawthorne's gallery and made off with the paintings in the first place. They never would because She. Hadn't. Done. It.

A wave washed over her toes as another gust of frigid air lashed at the lapels of her sweater. Sunny jumped back from the icy water and, crossing her arms over her midsection, turned for her temporary home. At the end of the wooden walkway leading from the beach to her dad's house, she picked up the canvas sneakers she'd left there then hurried past the pool, closed for the winter, and onto the covered deck. A wall of wind-driven rain drove her inside.

She cleaned her feet then flicked the switch to turn on the gas fireplace. After fixing herself a mug of hot chocolate, complete with mini marshmallows, she curled on the sofa facing the fire. She'd never minded being alone until she'd spent most of a week with Jake Ingram. Now, she couldn't seem to settle. She tried reading but gave up after staring at the same page for untold minutes. Even her favorite TV shows didn't hold her attention. She was contemplating the movie offerings on a satellite subscription service when her cell phone rang.

Her best friend, Melody Travis, called her frequently since Sunny's arrest and release on bail. Apparently, the fiasco made national news. Mel and her husband, rock star Hank Travis, coincidentally, an old friend of Jake's, offered their support from the get-go. They'd even suggested she come stay with them but apologized when they realized what they'd offered. No way could she hide out in the man's hometown they'd accused her of stealing from. And she especially couldn't hide out in the home of one of his friends.

Sunny picked up on the second ring.

"Melody, hi. How are things in Texas?"

Mel filled Sunny in on her perfect husband and her more perfect daughter, Gloria. Sunny didn't mind. It did more to take her mind off her troubles than anything else she'd tried lately.

"How are things with you? Any news?" Mel asked when she wound down.

"No. I'm still the prime suspect. I don't think the police are looking for the actual culprits."

"They can't convict you without proof, can they?"

"My lawyer seems to think otherwise. I don't have an alibi for the day they stole the paintings. Apparently, being sick as a dog and spending the day at home alone isn't considered an alibi."

"But there's no motive!" Mel cried over the line. "Why would you steal awful paintings?"

Suddenly, she had Sunny's full attention. "You've seen them?"

"Yeah." Sunny thought she could have heard her friend's sigh all the way from Texas without aid of a phone. "Will invited us to his bonfire last night. I got a good look at them before he torched them."

Sunny gasped. "He really burned them?"

"To cinders. There's a video. I sent you a copy. Watch it then call me."

"Okay. I'll call you right back."

Her phone dinged, showing she'd received a text message. She opened it and waited for the extensive video file to download.

CHAPTER SEVENTEEN

Before she finished watching the video, several more text messages arrived from her dad and her lawyer. She ignored them, mesmerized by the flames and hoping desperately to get a glimpse of Jake. When nothing but embers remained, Will made another statement then the camera panned over the small group gathered to witness the destruction of the paintings. When Jake's face filled the frame, Sunny paused the video, staring at the man who owned her heart.

Tears streamed down her cheeks. She wiped them away with the flat of her hand. He was still as handsome as ever, but there was a tension in his features she didn't recall. He looked…tired. Stressed. Like he hadn't been sleeping well. "Welcome to the crowd," she mumbled, pressing the button to restart the video.

As she'd promised, she placed a call to Melody Travis. "Hey, it's me."

"Did you watch it?"

"From start to finish," she confirmed. "It was hard to watch."

"Tell me about it. It's something I'll never forget."

"Will seemed determined. How was he off camera?"

"For someone who torched over a year of his own work, worth an estimated cool million? He seemed relieved. He served champagne and had some of his recent work on display. Based on what I saw before he burned them, I can tell you, they weren't anything like the ones I bought from you a few years ago. Those are masterpieces. The burned ones? Not so much. I'm no art critic, so I'm probably using the wrong words, but I'd say they had no soul."

"What about the new ones he displayed?"

"Is magnificent a word you use in the art world? Is there something more descriptive? I'd trade my husband for one of them, and you know how I feel about Hank. They're that good."

"You didn't take any pictures, did you?"

"What kind of idiot do you think I am? Of course I did. I'm sending them now."

Sunny's phone vibrated. She opened the text app and pulled up the photos. "Wow. They're stunning."

"Stunning. Magnificent. Museum quality."

"I'm so glad he's painting again, and his work is even better than before." She'd love to get her hands on one of them for her own collection. "What does he plan to do with them?"

"He said they aren't for sale. But he mentioned he was working on another one he planned to put up for auction. Sotheby's offered to handle the sale without taking their cut."

Sunny's head spun. "Can you let me know when that happens?"

"I told him to give me a heads-up. Are you going to bid against me?"

"Probably." Given her infamous connection to the artist, she'd need to have her lawyer bid on her behalf.

"Be prepared to pay up then because, sight unseen, I want whatever he's painting."

"With the notoriety around his name, lots of art collectors are going to be interested. The price will skyrocket."

"I figured as much. I'll have to determine how high I'm willing to go and maybe enter a maximum bid beforehand."

A maximum bid would keep a bidder in the running up until the bids exceeded the predetermined ceiling. It was a safeguard used by many collectors to keep from getting caught up in the excitement and paying too much for a single item. She'd used the strategy before but knew she'd do no such thing for this auction. "That's an excellent idea. I've got a feeling this one will be wild."

"Speaking of wild, how are you *really* doing? Don't bullshit me, girlfriend. I can tell when you are.

Sunny closed her eyes. The concern in her friend's voice brought fresh tears to the surface which only added to her frustration. "The truth is, I'm a basket case. I can't sleep. I can't eat. All I do is cry. The police aren't even looking for anyone else!" She broke down and sobbed. "How is this my life?"

"Oh, honey, I'm so sorry. What about the PI you hired?"

"He hasn't had any luck, either. It's like Cecil and Jessica dropped off the face of the earth. How is that even possible?"

"I have no idea. New identities, maybe? I've hidden behind a different name before, remember? I used my mom's family name most of my life. I bought my house here in Willowbrook through a corporation I set up to hide my involvement. What did they do with the money they stole from Will's bank accounts? They didn't give it back, so it must be somewhere. Did they get it in cash? Or was it transferred to another account?"

Sunny's ears perked. Melody's father was a legendary rock star who died when she was young. To avoid the spotlight, she'd claimed her mother's family name as her own until a few years ago when her identity became public. Sunny's dad used a fake name to check into hotels all the time. "You're right. They're probably using fake names, and the money has to be somewhere. I wonder if Jake's PI tried to trace it. I wonder if mine has?"

"Ask, girlfriend. There's a lot on the line here. You need to clear your name."

"I don't want to go to jail."

"That's the spirit. Hey, if you need me to come hold your hand, just say the word. Gloria and I will fire up the jet and be there in a few hours."

Smiling for the first time since her arrest, she laughed. Her friend would use any excuse to bring her toddler daughter to New York for a shopping trip. "I appreciate your willingness to leave your hunky husband, but I'm fine. I need to be proactive. Get the charges dropped and clear my name, once and for all. Then we'll shop until our credit cards cry, Uncle! Deal?"

"Deal, girlfriend. But the offer still stands. Anytime."

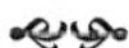

They'd become a tabloid sensation.

Will's video, despite its extended length, went viral. Even though MacKenzie offered to handle PR for him in her spare time, he'd hired a firm out of Dallas to deal with requests for interviews and to monitor his social media accounts.

Jake dropped a copy of a national scandal sheet on his desk. Ever since it hit the newsstands, his phones, business and personal, had been ringing constantly. He'd silenced his cell phone and blocked dozens of numbers in a matter of hours, and he'd instructed his admin not to answer the office line unless she knew the person calling in.

He should sue the rag for the story they'd printed about him and Sunny. However, most of what they'd printed was true. They'd done their research and come up with a detailed timeline for the days he and the gallery owner, now the prime suspect in the theft of his brother's paintings, spent in upstate New York. They'd even interviewed the chicken farmers!

The reporter drew some accurate conclusions about what the two of them had been up to during the times they couldn't be accounted for and the night they'd spent at the bed-and-breakfast. The one thing they hadn't uncovered was the night they'd spent at Ross McClelland's house or why they'd been in Scranton, the morning before Sunny's arrest at her Manhattan brownstone. It was only a matter of time, Jake concluded, before they came up with the rest of the story.

Jake picked up the phone to warn Ross what was headed his way. The old man answered on the third ring.

"Jake. Hey, I heard the news about Ms. Sheldon. It's bullshit, of course."

He wasn't so sure, but he hadn't called to debate Sunny's guilt or innocence. "A lot has happened since we were at your house. I thought I'd warn you. The tabloids have gotten their hooks into the story. One of them has a reporter tracing every step Sunny and I took the week we came to see you. So far, they've stopped short of calling our relationship a conspiracy to undermine my brother's career, but if they could find a scrap of evidence to support it, I'm sure they would. So…just be aware if someone comes snooping around."

"I get it. You'd rather I not comment."

"That's not what I'm saying. Be straight with them, but you know how those rags are. If a nun says she's married to Christ, they'll drag God and the holy spirit into it and call it an orgy."

The former PR guru laughed. "You're right. I think it's best to stick with no comment. If they find me. I'm far off-the-grid. You didn't tell anyone where you were going or that you'd been here, did you?"

"No, I didn't. But I can't vouch for Sunny. We parted on less-than-friendly terms."

"I'm real sorry to hear that. You don't believe what they're saying about her, do you?"

Jake sighed and scrubbed his free hand over his face. "I don't want to, but the evidence doesn't lie, Ross."

"Fuck the evidence—pardon my French. She loves art. She's devoted her career to helping young artists make a name for themselves. She'd never steal from anyone, let alone an artist with the promise your brother shows." He paused. Jake could hear him coughing in the background. Then he came back on the line. "Don't be stupid, boy. She loves you.

Take it from someone who knows, you only get so many days with the ones you love. Don't waste them."

The line went silent. "Hello? Ross? Are you there?" Jake took the phone from his ear, glared at the words on the screen. Call Ended. "He hung up on me. The old bastard hung up on me." He dropped his phone on top of the tabloid with his picture front and center.

"Shit."

The rest of the day, McClelland's words echoed in his brain. She'd never steal from anyone. *Don't be stupid, boy. She loves you.*

Was she capable of stealing? Even Will didn't think she'd stolen his paintings. Yesterday, Melody Travis called to chastise him for abandoning Sunny to the tabloids, claiming her friend had done nothing but try to help him find the people who wronged his brother. According to her, Sunny was holed up at her dad's house in the Hamptons, afraid to even return to her own home. He couldn't reconcile the image with the one he had of the woman. The Sunny Sheldon he knew wasn't afraid of anything.

His body hardened at the thought of all the places and ways they'd made love on their road trip. She'd given herself to him in a clearing in the freakin' woods. Twice. And then there was the time she gave him a blow job in the car, in a restaurant parking lot. Talk about fearless.

But it had all been a distraction. A way to keep him from discovering the truth.

Was he being stupid? Did she love him?

He closed his eyes, recalling his brother's latest painting. The nude of MacKenzie where more than her body was exposed. In fact, her physical nudity was the last thing he noticed. Her expression, the love apparent in the depth of her gaze, had captured his attention first. It drew him in instantly because he'd seen that look before. Sunny gazed at him in the same way, and he'd felt the power of her emotion down to his toes and returned it in equal measure.

Jake's entire body shook as his newfound awareness hit

him full force. Sunny loved him. And he loved her. And, he'd left her at the mercy of a rabid press and a police department eager to close a case.

The realization nearly brought him to his knees.

He spun his chair around to peer out the window. Heat shimmered off the earth's surface giving the landscape a surreal presence. Jake narrowed his gaze to a garden gnome, a gift a few years ago from his administrative assistant. A joke gift that appeared in the garden alcove, holding a balloon bouquet on his birthday. The balloons were long since gone, but the statue remained.

He'd screwed up. Let Sunny down and, by extension, his brother. Getting Will's money and paintings back wasn't the end of it. He'd still been wronged, and convicting the wrong person wouldn't serve justice. Wouldn't provide the closure his brother deserved.

And Sunny didn't deserve to suffer for something she didn't do. She was as much a victim as Will. Maybe more so because the actual culprits had targeted her to take the blame for their crimes.

"Why would anyone want to hurt her?" he asked the grinning gnome. "What did she do to them?" He stood to pace the length of his office. "Had destroying her been part of the plan all along? Leave her holding the bag for the art heist while Hawthorne and Blackwell got away with the money?"

"Don't forget Ginger Carpenter, Sunny's part-time salesperson."

Jake glared at his middle brother who lounged in the open doorway. "Eavesdropping, Bro?"

"No. Your door was open." Will strode in like he belonged and took a seat facing Jake's desk. "You talk to yourself often?"

After dropping into his desk chair, Jake propped his feet on his desk. "Sometimes, it's the only way to have an intelligent conversation."

Will shrugged. "As long as you don't answer yourself, I

guess it's okay." His mischievous smile reminded Jake of when they were kids. Will was always coming up with a plan guaranteed to get the three of them in trouble. "You don't answer yourself, do you?"

Jake grinned. "Like I said, it's a surefire way to have an intelligent conversation." Placing his elbows on the arms of his chair, he steepled his fingers, studying his nails. "What do you know about Ginger Carpenter?"

"Nope. Not telling you anything until you tell me why you were pacing and asking yourself questions about my case."

He dropped his feet to the floor, leaned into his desk. "Sunny didn't steal your paintings."

"What makes you think so?"

"I know her. She's not a criminal. Think about it. She doesn't have the money from your accounts, and she'd have to be stupid to sell stolen paintings out of her gallery."

"Do you know where the money went? Maybe she was working with Jessica all along and they split the money. Put it in offshore accounts. And someone did sell one of the paintings at her gallery."

Dumbfounded by Will's about-face where Sunny was concerned, he lit into him. "What's gotten into you? Do you know something I don't? If you do, you'd better tell me now before I knock some sense into you."

Will doubled over, laughing. "Oh, man. You've got it bad." He slapped his knee. "Never thought I would see the mighty Jake Ingram fall for a woman, but it's happened. You're in love with her, aren't you?"

"Fuck you." Jake stood, ready to beat the shit out of his brother. "Sunny did nothing wrong, and I intend to prove it. You can help me, or you can go fuck yourself."

"Stand down, Bro." Will raised his hand in surrender. "I was trying to get your goat. See how committed you are to getting answers to the questions you were asking yourself."

"Why the hell didn't you just ask, asswipe?" He sat, picked up a pen, then slid a yellow note pad front and center.

"If you have nothing helpful to contribute, get the hell out. I have work to do."

CHAPTER EIGHTEEN

Jake tossed his pen down then rocked back in his chair. Rubbing his eyes with the heels of his hands, he groaned. He brought himself upright and surveyed the damage. Coffee cups and note pads, many sporting brown rings and coffee splatters, littered his desk. "Looks like we pulled an all-nighter," he commented to his brother who'd given up on the uncomfortable visitors' chair hours ago and was now stretched out on the sofa across the room.

Will shifted to a sitting position, resting his elbows on his knees, hands clasped in front. "What time is it?"

"Past time to go home." He consulted his watch. "If we hurry, we can grab a bite at the diner before it closes."

Stretching his arms above his head as he stood, Will replied, "Don't have to tell me twice."

The brothers walked the single block to the local establishment they'd eaten at since they were kids. At this hour, the place was empty, except for a few locals having pie and coffee at the counter. Jake led the way to a booth next to the window, close enough the sole waitress wouldn't have far to walk yet far enough away from the other customers to carry on a conversation without being overheard.

Given the late hour, they both waved off the offered caffeine, choosing large glasses of milk instead to go with the hearty breakfast platters they ordered. "Did we accomplish anything at all?" Will asked when they were alone.

"Maybe." Jake downed half his milk to appease his protesting stomach. He wasn't sure how much of his problem was lack of food and how much resulted from all the coffee he'd consumed. "I'll call Philip in the morning," he said, referencing the PI he'd worked with in New York. "Last time I talked to him I was pissed off and told him to quit looking. I'll see if he can pick up where he left off. If not, I'll find someone who can, or I'll go back and do it myself."

"Maybe you should go back anyway. See Sunny. Try to explain your behavior."

He doubted she wanted to hear anything he had to say. His stomach felt like it was twisting into a knot. He took a tiny sip of his milk. "You think that's wise?"

"Why wouldn't it be?"

"If I were her attorney, I'd tell her to stay the hell away from anyone associated with the case."

"Do your clients listen when you tell them shit like that?"

"No." He drained his glass, setting it on the edge of the table as a silent signal for a refill. "They usually go out and do exactly the opposite."

"There you go." Will saluted with his beverage then took a sip. "If nothing else, she'll want to tell you off for abandoning her to the police."

The server set another glass of milk on the table. "Food's almost ready," she said, taking the empty glass with her as she left.

"You've got a point." He stared at the ancient Formica tabletop. "I really fucked this up."

"She'll understand...eventually."

Jake huffed out a laugh. Glancing up, he caught his brother's smirk. "Asshole."

"Hey, what are brothers for? You don't want me to sugarcoat it, do you? You acted like a jerk, now you're going to have to make amends."

"In other words, I need to clear her name then beg her to listen."

"Beg being the operative word."

"Maybe you can give me pointers on begging. I've never done it before."

"Now who's being an asshole?"

Their food arrived, putting an end to the banter. Once their plates were empty, they relaxed, arms stretched across the back of the booth. Will nudged Jake's foot under the table. "So, when are you leaving?"

"Don't know. Depends on what the PI has, and I have work I need to finish up. Maybe day after tomorrow?"

"I could go with you."

"Nah. No need for you to get tangled up in this mess again." Jake leaned forward, wrapped his hands around his glass. "I'm thinking this never really was about you. If it was, why go after Sunny now?"

"You think they stole my money and my paintings in some sick game to damage Sunny's reputation?"

"I know it sounds nuts, but how is it any crazier than them targeting you in the first place?"

Will picked up his fork, used it to draw lines in the syrup left behind on his plate. When the grooves filled in, he repeated the process. "You could be right, but there must be a reason they chose me and not some other schmuck."

"I can't come up with a reason to target you or Sunny. None of this makes any sense." They'd been over every scrap of information, spouted out every theory and a few impossible ones over the course of the afternoon. As tired as they both were, nothing would be gained by rehashing everything tonight.

Will picked up the check the server had left on the table, examined it. "I appreciate all you've done for me. I was in a bad place when I came home. Broke. Broken. You never questioned how I got myself into such a mess, you just jumped in and worked the problem. Thanks to you, my money was returned and those damn paintings won't be coming back to haunt me years from now." He creased the paper in his hands then smoothed it out. "I'm sorry you got dragged into this but at the same time, I'm grateful you did."

"I probably wouldn't have ever met Sunny if it weren't for you and your screwed-up life, so I should be grateful you let me help you." Jake straightened the flatware dropped haphazardly on his plate. "I love her, Will." He looked up, locked gazes with his brother. "I'll do whatever it takes to get her out of this mess."

"I know you will." He held up the bill. "I've got this, Bro."

Jake nodded. "Tip's on me." He pulled a couple of bills from his wallet, tossed them on the table.

They made the short walk to Jake's office in silence. Will waved as he left the parking lot. Jake returned to his office to turn out lights and secure his files. He crammed the notes he'd scribbled earlier into his briefcase. At home, he poured himself two fingers of his best whiskey and sat down to prioritize the questions they'd come up with.

Top of the list—Who was Ginger Carpenter, and how was she involved with Cecil Hawthorne and Jessica Blackwell?

❦

"You sure you don't want me to come with you?" Will asked as he pulled Jake's car to the curb.

"I appreciate the offer, but like I tell all my clients, let me handle it. It's what you pay me for."

"If that's a subtle way of telling me I'm going to have to pay you, think again." His brother shoved the gearshift into Park.

Jake popped the passenger-side door open, slid his right foot to the pavement, ignoring his brother's attempt at humor. "Don't wreck my car on the way home, asshole." He slammed the door shut, opened the rear door, and yanked his carry-on out. He leaned into the car. "I'll call when I have something to report."

Will craned his head around. "Text me when you land. Believe it or not, Rick and I worry about you."

Not as much as I worry about the two of you. "Yes, Mom," he said, slamming the door. Turning his back on his brother, he entered the terminal. He hadn't heard from his PI since yesterday morning when he'd given him another list of things to check out. Waiting at the gate, he phoned the NYPD detective in charge of the case but ended up having to leave a voice message.

Technically, Jake had done his job. He'd made sure Will's funds and property were returned to him. He could walk away now, let the police and prosecutors do their job, but his gut told him Sunny wasn't guilty of anything, except maybe hiring the wrong person to help at her gallery. He'd gone over the original police reports and discovered they'd never interviewed Ginger Carpenter about the heist, leaving her free to carry out the third leg of the crime—frame Sunny Sheldon.

He didn't want to throw shade on any law enforcement, but he suspected they hadn't interviewed her about the sale of the stolen painting, either. When he'd spoken to Detective Reeves outside Sunny's brownstone the day they arrested her, he'd mentioned the buyer's description of the woman who introduced herself as Sunny Sheldon. Called it a slam-dunk. Eager to close the case, he probably hadn't bothered to question the woman's memory. Jake wasn't even sure he'd asked if Sunny could provide an alibi.

As soon as the wheels touched the runway at JFK, Jake checked his messages. There was one from the PI. After texting Will and Rick to let them know he'd landed safely, he listened to his voicemail.

"Good morning, Mr. Ingram. This is Philip Holland. I've got some information for you regarding the person of interest you contacted me about. Please call me." He rattled off his phone number. Jake ended the recitation. He'd rather hear what the man found out in person. Carry-on in hand, he hopped into the first available cab and gave the driver the

PI's address.

If the PI was surprised to see Jake, he hid it well. The two men shook hands. " "Come on back to my office." The private investigator shut the door then took a seat behind his desk. He opened a folder. "You asked me to find anything I could on a Ginger Carpenter employed by Sunnyside Gallery in Manhattan."

Jake nodded. "What did you find out?"

"Ginger is her stage name. Landed a few bit parts on Broadway, but most of her credits are for off-Broadway productions. Small stuff. Nothing anyone has ever heard of. She auditions for any and everything. Plays, musicals, commercials, TV shows, movies. Her agent says she hasn't found the right vehicle for her brand of talent, which is entertainment speak for she's unmarketable."

Jake nodded his understanding. "She has no talent."

"Exactly."

"Go on."

Philip consulted his report. "To make ends meet, and I use the term loosely, she works multiple part-time retail jobs. The longest, by far, is her time with Sunnyside Gallery. She's been there for several years."

"Do you have an address for her?"

"I do, but she no longer lives there."

"Why not?"

"I spoke to the property owner. Her name wasn't on the lease, but he remembered her. He was about to evict her for nonpayment when she disappeared."

"Whose name was on the lease?"

"Cecil Hawthorne."

Jake stared across the desk at the PI. "Seriously?"

"I have a copy of the lease. Shitty place, too. If she was sleeping with him, she should have demanded better accommodations."

"When did she skip out?"

The PI consulted his papers, named a date.

"That's a few days after the sale of my brother's stolen

painting." Jake filled the PI in on the developments regarding the missing paintings on the same day he'd informed him to quit looking for Hawthorne and Blackwell. "Where has she been for the weeks between now and then?"

"I spoke with the building superintendent. Asked if he'd seen anything unusual. He mentioned seeing her and a guy meeting Hawthorne's description hauling a bunch of canvases up the three flights of stairs months ago. Never saw them leave, but he wasn't watching her apartment. It's only luck he was there the day she moved them in. The property owner told me she'd left everything behind, except for her clothes. I asked about the paintings. He assured me there were a few cheap prints on the walls and nothing else. Which bears out since your brother's paintings turned up elsewhere."

Jake slumped in his chair. "Well, now we know where the paintings were all this time."

"The question is, why? If they were worth as much as everyone assumed, why did Hawthorne give them to her?"

"Assuming he did so willingly?"

Philip shrugged. "Or not so willingly." He steepled his fingers in front of his face. "They could have been payment for something. Services rendered or perhaps blackmail. Maybe he gave them to her in exchange for keeping her mouth shut."

"She had to have known stolen paintings weren't worth anything except a prison sentence," Jake surmised.

"Unless you have another use for them." The PI turned a few pages over, scanned the page he'd found. "Here's the interesting part." He smiled a cat-with-a-canary smile. "Care to guess what Ginger Carpenter's actual name is?"

"Son of a bitch."

"My thoughts, exactly." Philip scribbled something on a piece of paper, slid it across the desk.

Jake took the note, eyed the address. "Whose place is

this?"

"Curtis Sheldon."

Nodding, Jake stood, offered his hand.

The PI did likewise then handed Jake the thick file folder. "Let me know if I can be of any more help."

On the sidewalk, Jake took a minute to get his bearings. Philip saved the best for last. Jake needed a few minutes to wrap his head around the new information and to come up with a plan. Spying a coffee shop down the block, he made his way there and ordered a giant cup of java and a slice of lemon pound cake. Luckily, most of the customers took theirs to go, leaving plenty of seats to choose from. Jake claimed a big leather chair in the corner and sat to enjoy the afternoon treat. While he ate, he read through the report. The PI was right. He needed to visit Mr. Sheldon before he did anything else.

Jake dismissed the Uber driver before he could change his mind about the path he'd chosen. The townhouse on the Upper East Side of Manhattan was impressive. The white marble facade boasted a lot of carved detail. About a dozen steps led up to a glossy black door embellished with a polished brass handle and door knocker. Colorful fall flowers adorned window boxes along the first-floor windows and others in pots lined the staircase. Everything about the place screamed money. With his overnighter still in hand, Jake climbed the steps to Curtis Sheldon's front door. As he pressed the doorbell, it occurred to him he didn't even know if the man was home. He could literally be anywhere in the world.

Hearing footsteps approaching, Jake squared his shoulders and cleared his throat. The door swung open. Jake recognized Sunny's father from the many movies he'd seen the man in over the years. Mr. Sheldon's gaze swept Jake from head to toe, paused a moment on the carry-on sitting next to him on the top step, then swung back to his face. "I don't care what you're selling. I don't want any."

Jake spoke up before the door fully closed in his face. "Mr. Sheldon. I'm here about your daughter, Samantha."

CHAPTER NINETEEN

The door swung wide again. Jake wasn't sure if the actor's expression was shock or anger. Perhaps some of both.

Sunny's father glared at him. "Who the hell are you?"

"Jake Ingram, sir. Your other daughter, Sunny, is accused of stealing my brother's paintings. I don't think she did it."

"Jake Ingram," he mused. "You're the lawyer?"

"Yes, sir."

He stepped back. "Come in before someone sees you."

Jake stepped into the spacious vestibule. From the outside, the place appeared small, but from the entryway, he could see all the way to the kitchen which occupied the back portion of the first floor. Although narrow, the townhouse had plenty of square footage if you considered the two floors above and one below. The modern décor suggested a recent update, but personal touches like family photos on the walls and a well-loved sofa made the home look lived in.

Mr. Sheldon shut and locked the door.

"Nice place," Jake said as he followed his host through to the kitchen where the actor waved him to a barstool at the large kitchen island.

Sunny's dad poured himself a cup of coffee from the pot of an aged coffeemaker out of place in the ultra-modern kitchen. "Coffee?"

Jake nodded. "Thanks." As the actor poured another cup and slid the mug across the counter to him, Jake fought the urge to laugh. Who would have thought Curtis Sheldon would serve him coffee? On what planet did something like this happen?

After ascertaining Jake took his coffee black, the older man leaned back against the counter, facing Jake. "What's this about Samantha?"

"Did you know she's been working as Sunny's assistant at the gallery for several years?"

Mr. Sheldon froze, his coffee almost to his lips. Slowly, he lowered the mug then gripped the edge of the soapstone on either side of him. "No, I didn't." His jaw clenched, and his knuckles grew white as he dug his fingers into the stone. Jake could see the wheels turning behind the man's astute eyes.

"She's been using her stage name, Ginger Carpenter."

"Fuck." Sunny's father spun, braced himself on the counter, his head hanging. Jake sipped his coffee, waiting for the man to regain his composure. His shocked reaction to Jake's statement confirmed his suspicion Sunny didn't know she had a sister. Half sister.

"Sunny doesn't know, does she?"

"No." The actor turned. He'd aged ten years in the last minute. Not a good sign. "I need to sit." He waved Jake to follow him. "Bring your coffee." Sunny's dad left his in the kitchen, opting for a shot of whiskey from the antique sideboard that doubled as a bar in the living area. After downing the shot, he poured two fingers into the cut-crystal tumbler. "Care for something stronger?"

"No, thanks. Coffee's fine."

Mr. Sheldon sat on one end of the sofa, kicked his feet up on the reclaimed wood coffee table. Jake took a seat on the opposite end and kept his feet on the floor. And waited. Curtis Sheldon was a brilliant man who used his intelligence to bring the characters he portrayed to life. He'd won the industry's highest awards on both screen and stage, though you wouldn't know it from looking at this portion of his home. Maybe he kept them in an office or at one of his other homes. Sunny mentioned her father owned a house in Los Angeles and the beach house in the Hamptons.

"Margery and I decided not to tell Sunny about her half sister when they were both infants."

"Margery is Sunny's mother?"

"Yes. My affair with Samantha's mother was the end of our marriage, though Marge is still the love of my life. I fucked it all up, literally. Marge could have forgiven me just about anything, but infidelity wasn't one of them."

"Sunny told me you and her mother were still in love but couldn't live with each other."

He stared at the brown liquid in his glass. "She's right. I've never loved anyone else. I've been with others over the years, but my heart still belongs to Margery. I never questioned why she didn't remarry."

"What about Samantha's mother?"

"Ginger?" Mr. Sheldon's gaze clouded. "She was a one-night stand. I was starring in a Broadway musical. Margery was pregnant with Sunny. Difficult pregnancy. On bedrest for months. Ginger was there. Part of the dance company—you know—extras that fill in the non-speaking parts. She was beautiful and spirited. Most of the extras were afraid to talk to the stars." He put the last word in air quotes. "But not Ginger. She was always hanging around. Learning from us, she said. I was lonely. That's not an excuse, just a fact. Margery was in California, and I was in New York. We talked on the phone, and I went to see her every chance I got, but my schedule didn't allow it often. Broadway is grueling. Eight live shows a week. The only way to get a night off is to be sick or pay the stand-in to go on for you. The show had just opened, and the producers frowned on the stars taking time off. People payed to see the big names, not the stand-ins."

The actor stood, refilled his glass, then paced to gaze out the window. "We'd accomplished a rare, perfect night on stage. Everyone was on. No one missed a line or a cue. The audience ate it up. I'd never taken as many curtain calls as I did that night. We threw a cast party afterward to celebrate. I drank too much. Might have been feeling sorry for myself because I didn't have anyone to celebrate with, if you get my meaning." He sipped his drink. "Ginger was there. Telling me everything I wanted Margery to be there telling me. Next thing I knew, we were in the prop room and my pants were around my ankles. I backed her up against the wall and fucked her. It was over in minutes. We straightened our clothes and went back to the party. Didn't talk about it again until a few weeks later when she told me she was pregnant.

"I almost had a heart attack. I knew I couldn't tell Margery, not until after she delivered. I agreed to pay all of Ginger's medical expenses. Set up a trust fund for the baby even before Samantha was born.

"Hardest thing I ever had to do was tell Margery what I'd done. Sunny was a year old, Samantha about six months old. Margery told me to get out. She never wanted to see me again. We've shared custody of Sunny from then on. Never disagreed about how to raise her."

"But you never told Sunny about her half sister."

"No. Margery and I decided she didn't need to know."

"What about Samantha? Obviously, she has known for a while."

Sunny's dad ran his free hand through his hair. "Ginger died about five years ago. Breast cancer. Her attorney notified me since I'd been financially supporting them for years. Samantha wasn't supposed to be told about me until she turned twenty-five and her trust fund was turned over to her. She was only about a year from reaching her majority, so I amended the trust to let her have access. I met with her a few times after that, always with our lawyers present. She wanted nothing to do with me, and I didn't try to convince her otherwise. I didn't want to rub Margie's face in my mistake, and I wasn't keen on telling Sunny how I'd screwed up."

"You haven't heard from Samantha in all this time?"

"No. Not a word. Occasionally, I'll see her stage name

listed in the supporting cast, mostly off-Broadway productions or mentioned in *Variety*. It always gives me a jolt, since she uses her mother's name. Seeing it brings back unpleasant memories. Anyway, Samantha made no attempt to contact me, and God forgive me, I didn't contact her, either. If what you say is true, my cowardice has come around to bite me in the ass."

"I have documentation of her employment at Sunnyside Gallery. The private investigator I hired spoke to her landlord and her building superintendent. The property owner confirmed Cecil Hawthorne paid her rent until he disappeared. They'd given her multiple eviction notices in the last few months. The building super said he saw her lugging a bunch of paintings up the stairs to her apartment about the time my brother's paintings went missing from Hawthorne's gallery."

"Yet, they turned up in the basement of Sunny's brownstone and the storeroom at the gallery."

Jake nodded. "Do you think Sunny would have given Ginger, I mean, Samantha, access to her home? I know she had a key to the gallery. Sunny mentioned calling her to have her open a few hours a day while the two of us were upstate."

Mr. Sheldon settled back on the sofa, placing his empty tumbler on the coffee table. "Let me guess. Samantha sold the painting, the one that led to Sunny's arrest? And now she's disappeared."

"Sounds like the plot of a really bad movie, but yeah, I think she pretended to be Sunny when she sold the painting. The PI gave me a picture of her. It wouldn't take much to pass herself off as Sunny, especially to someone who didn't know her. Side by side, I think I'd notice the resemblance, though, not knowing their actual relationship, I doubt I'd make the connection."

"I need to tell Sunny."

"And the cops."

Sunny's dad rested his forearms on his thighs, clasped his hands in front. His head hung between his shoulders. "One stupid mistake three decades ago. I need to call Margery. Give her a heads-up. This will cause a media frenzy. My agent is going to kill me."

Jake ignored his self-pity party. He couldn't count how many times he'd heard similar laments, minus the PR nightmare, from his clients, both male and female. Marital mistakes were a dime a dozen no matter what your profession. Still, he found it difficult to feel sorry for the man. If he'd come clean from the beginning, told Sunny and Samantha, perhaps built a genuine relationship with both, fostered one between the sisters, things would have turned out differently.

Jake stood, helped himself to two fingers of the man's excellent bourbon. He fortified himself with a sip before making his request. "I want to be there when you tell Sunny."

The declaration brought the actor's head up. He studied Jake like he was memorizing everything about him in order to play him onstage. "You broke her heart."

The older man's barb hit him hard, buried under his skin. "I made a mistake. I'm willing to admit it and live with the consequences."

"Why didn't you leave this alone? As I understand it, your brother got his money and his paintings back. Why not let the NYPD think they'd solved the case?"

"I thought about it, sir. I thought your daughter lied to me. Betrayed my family. It took me a while, but I came to my senses and realized Sunny isn't stupid. She'd never sell a stolen painting, much less one she knew everyone in the art world would be on the lookout for."

"The police think differently."

"I know her better than they do."

Mr. Sheldon stood. "How well do you know her?"

The weight of the concerned father's stare made him feel like a bug under a microscope. Jake took another sip from his glass. The aged bourbon burned a trail all the way to his stomach. Liquid courage. "I know her well enough. Better than you knew Ginger Carpenter." He drew a fortifying breath and spoke from his heart. "I'm in love with her, sir. If she's anything like her mother, she probably won't forgive me, but if she will, I'll do whatever it takes to make her happy for the rest of her life."

CHAPTER TWENTY

"Wait here while I make a few phone calls. This might take a while, so make yourself at home. Rec room's in the basement."

Jake let out a pent-up breath as Curtis Sheldon, possibly his future father-in-law, disappeared up the staircase, leaving him to his own devices. At least he hadn't punched him for the veiled reference he'd made to the older man's decades-old fuckup, or to the inference of an intimate relationship with the man's daughter. Jake's statement of intent where Sunny was concerned gained him a grudging smile from her father. Facing off with the famous actor felt surreal. Jake could admit to himself he'd been a little intimidated by the man, not because of his fame but because of the influence he held over his daughter. One word from him, and Sunny might never forgive him.

With an unknown amount of time to kill, Jake made his way around the room, checking out the framed photos. Most were casual snapshots of him and Sunny taken at recognizable tourist spots around the world. A few were of him and other easily recognizable actors on a boat, showing off their catch. He couldn't believe these were the people Sunny and her dad called friends. Surreal. If Sunny forgave him, he hoped to become a permanent part of her world—a world he knew nothing about.

Having examined everything on public display, he ventured down the stairs to see what passed for a rec room in the world of the rich and famous. He stopped on the last stair tread and stared. Talk about a man cave. A giant screen TV occupied an entire wall, while a giant trophy fish claimed another. A grouping of overstuffed sofas and chairs provided enough lounge space for a football team. A pool table and various electronic games occupied one corner, and a massive wet bar completed the dream space. Jake expected the basement to be dark and cramped, but this one was bright as day, lit with subtle lighting that bounced off walls painted off-white to match the rugs scattered over the hardwood floors.

He forced his feet to move. Found a massive remote on the coffee table. After spending a few minutes guessing at which button to push first, he found one that looked promising. The giant screen came to life with a menu. From there, it was easy enough to maneuver through the channels to find a baseball game already in progress. Didn't matter who was playing. Even when he'd been playing football in high school, he'd preferred to watch baseball. Turned out, he didn't have the hand/eye coordination to play the game at anything beyond a rec level, but the complexity of it appealed to him.

Jake muted the game then grabbed a soda from the well-stocked bar. After settling into the inviting sofa, he placed a call to Will.

"Hey. You'll never guess where I am." He spent the next half hour catching his brother up on everything he'd found out since arriving in New York. "He's making some phone calls. His ex and Sunny. Don't know if he'll get her to come here or if we're going out to the Hamptons to talk to her. I'll keep you informed." He shifted into big brother mode. "How's everything there?"

"I finished the painting I was working on. Might start another one tomorrow if I don't have to finish up work on Rick's latest project."

Their youngest brother's home remodel business had taken off in the last few months. Last Jake heard, Rick was booked up through the new year with jobs both big and small. "What do you mean? Why can't Rick finish it up?"

"He's not here." Until Will found a place of his own, he was still bunking with Rick at the house they'd grown up in.

"What do you mean, not here? Where is he?"

"He left right after I got home from dropping you at the airport. Said his Marine buddy was in Dallas again and he was going to go see him. I thought he'd be home by now, that's all. I'm sure he'll realize it's getting late and drag his ass home soon."

Rick had mentioned this friend several times, but Jake couldn't recall hearing the guy's name. His brother had been in such a funk when he left the Marines and returned home, Jake hadn't pressed him for details about his service. Now, he wished he had. "If you don't hear from him soon, let me know. Okay?"

"Okay, but what are you going to do about it from New York?"

Will had a point. Jake sighed and rubbed at the knot forming at the back of his neck. "I don't know, Will. One problem at a time, Brother."

"Don't worry about Rick. He's a grown man. He can take care of himself. Probably a hell of a lot better than either of us. Focus on getting Sunny to forgive you. You deserve some happiness, Jake."

"Yeah, well, even if she forgives me and we get her name cleared, I don't know how a relationship with her would work. We live in two different worlds."

"Call me a romantic, but I'm a firm believer love always finds a way."

"You've let your happiness with MacKenzie go to your head." Footsteps on the stairs reminded him why he was here. He rubbed at his neck again. The pain crept up the back of his skull. "Gotta go. I'll keep you informed."

❧

Sunny was used to her dad's unexpected visits. Given his celebrity status, he preferred to be spontaneous, rarely announcing his plans to anyone ahead of time. Since this was his house, he didn't bother to knock, just walked right in, as usual. At least this time, probably because of the late hour, he announced his presence immediately instead of scaring the bejesus out of her. Hearing him call her name, she grabbed a sweater off the chair next to the bed and bounded down the stairs to meet him.

"Hey, Dad," she called out, "what are you…?" The sight of the man standing behind her father robbed her of speech. The last time she'd seen Jake Ingram had been the day of her arrest. She'd found out later he'd known what was about to happen and been a willing participant in the day's festivities. His betrayal was still a boiling cauldron making her sick to her stomach and keeping her awake nights.

"Sunny." Her dad drew her attention. "We need to talk."

His words and solemn demeanor helped her find her voice. "I have nothing to say to him." She nodded at Jake.

"He might have something to say to you later on, but first, you need to hear what I have to say."

The sadness in his voice broke through the anguish squeezing her heart. She turned her gaze to her dad, only then noticing the red rims around his eyes and the deep lines formed around his mouth. She took the last few steps, stopping to embrace her dad. "What's wrong? Is Mom okay?"

"Your mom is fine. I spoke to her before I left to come see you. She sends her love and said to expect a call from her in the morning. She also said you can call her anytime if you want to talk."

Despite his reassurances, she couldn't help feeling like he was about to yank the rug out from under her feet. Dread gripped her in a cold vise. She wrapped her arms around her midsection, willing the bad mojo to go away. "I could use some hot tea. Let's go into the kitchen."

She led the way. The two men took seats at the island. While the kettle heated, she put out a plate of cookies she'd made earlier, for lack of something better to do. For the life of her, she couldn't imagine why Jake was here, with her father, no less. How did that happen? The more she thought about it, the more she became convinced this had to do with her arrest. From the expression on both their faces, it couldn't be good. Even more reason to postpone this talk as long as possible.

When they all had cups of tea, and there wasn't anything more she could do to stall the inevitable, she dragged a stool around the corner of the island where she could see them and sat. "Okay. What's this all about?"

"I understand you have an assistant by the name of Ginger Carpenter."

Sunny wrapped her chilled hands around her mug. The heat helped thaw her fingers and her nerves. "Yes. She's been with me as a part-time employee for about five years now. Why? Did something happen to her?" Suddenly, her hands were cold again.

"She's fine. As far as I know. But Jake here"—he hitched a thumb at the silent man beside him—"uncovered something that might clear you of all charges."

Sunny snapped her gaze to Jake. His eyes locked with hers, and, for a brief second, she was back in the clearing with him, their bodies moving as one, with so many unspoken words between them. Shaking her head, she broke the connection, giving her dad her full attention once again. "What did he find, and what does it have to do with Ginger?"

Her dad's gaze drifted to the steaming mug in his hands. "Maybe I should start at the beginning."

She nodded. "Okay."

"Your mom and I broke up because I had an affair. A one-night stand, actually."

Sunny listened to her dad's recitation of the events leading up to the demise of his marriage. What this had to do with Ginger or anything else, besides the fact both her parents lied to her for her entire life, she didn't know. Eventually, he got around to mentioning the woman's name.

"Wait a minute. Her name was Ginger Carpenter?"

"Yes. It was once, Sunny. We had no feelings for each other, not like your mom and I did before I ruined it."

"Mom wouldn't forgive you?"

"She might have if it ended there, but Ginger became pregnant. With my child."

"Oh. My. God." The puzzle pieces fell into place creating an awful picture she didn't want to see. "My assistant, Ginger Carpenter, is my sister?"

Her dad nodded once and, with a shaking hand, raised his mug to his lips. He took a sip then raised his eyes to hers once again. "Ginger Carpenter is her stage name, an homage to her mother, I guess. The name on her birth certificate is Samantha Sheldon."

It was almost too much to comprehend. She'd known Ginger for years, and they'd often joked about their uncanny resemblance. Had Ginger known all along they were related? "How long has she known we were sisters?"

"She found out about five years ago, when her mother died."

"Why wouldn't she say something?"

"I don't know. But Jake here found out some things. I'll let him tell you."

She still didn't see what any of this had anything to do with her being suspected of selling stolen property, but she was curious enough to hear what Jake had to say. She turned her attention to the man who, despite his betrayal, owned her heart. "I'm listening."

"Ginger is nowhere to be found. Disappeared when you and I were upstate looking for answers. Turns out, the answers were back in Manhattan. The PI I hired tracked down her landlord, found out he'd been trying to evict her for months for nonpayment. The apartment she occupied was leased to Cecil Hawthorne. He quit paying rent the same month Jessica disappeared."

Sunny held her hand up like a stop sign. She closed her eyes and shook her head. "Wait a second." She popped her eyes open, stared at Jake. "Ginger and Cecil? Are you kidding me?"

"No. There's more if you're ready to hear it."

She huffed out a laugh. "By all means, continue."

"The PI also talked to the building super. He said he helped Ginger carry a bunch of paintings up the stairs to her apartment about the time Will's paintings went missing from Hawthorne's gallery."

She didn't know what to say. She'd known and trusted Ginger for years. It was beyond comprehension the woman could be involved with something like this.

Jake grabbed one of her homemade cookies and bit into it. He washed the bite down with a swig of his tea. "We think Ginger pretended to be you when she sold Will's stolen painting. The two of you look enough alike, a stranger, someone who'd only met one of you, would months later provide a vague enough description to the police to make them think she'd interacted with you. And since Ginger is MIA, a side-by-side comparison is impossible."

"We joked about our resemblance. I thought it was funny, you know? We were rarely in the gallery at the same time, and when we were, I was usually in my office doing paperwork while she covered the sales floor. A time or two, customers would see us both and ask if we were sisters. We both laughed it off. Now, you're telling me she knew we were related and said nothing?"

"It looks that way," Jake confirmed. "Did you ever give her a key to your house, or could she have made a copy of your key?"

Sunny sipped her tea, giving the question time to sink in. "I didn't give her a key, but there was a day last year… We were crazy busy. We had a big shipment going out the next day, so I took some shipping orders home the night before to finish up and forgot to bring them in. To save time, Ginger offered to go get them while I finished the other paperwork. I gave her my keys and wrote the alarm code down for her."

"That answers the question of how the paintings ended up in your basement. She must have made a duplicate key, and you'd handed her the alarm code."

"And she already had access to the gallery. I know every inch of the storeroom there. Those paintings were not there the day you and I left on our trip. I'm certain. She had to have brought them in while we were away." She folded her arms on the island and dropped her forehead to her crossed arms. "I can't believe this."

The sound of chair legs scraping on the floor had her sitting up. Her dad stood beside the island. "I don't care how late it is, I'll call Detective Reeves. Now that we know how she got into your house, we need to turn this all over to him. This should be enough to clear your name."

That was the best news she'd heard in months. "God, I hope so." Relieved her ordeal might end soon, she waited until her dad turned down the hallway, out of sight. Feeling the heat of Jake's gaze on her back, she faced him. "You didn't have to follow up on this, but I'm grateful you did."

CHAPTER TWENTY-ONE

Jake dropped his gaze to his now-disgustingly cool tea. The last few months had taken a toll on Sunny, but she was still the most beautiful woman he'd ever seen. Always would be. He hoped she could forgive him for doubting her, for believing she could have done the things they accused her of. Glancing up, he met her gaze head-on. "I'm sorry, Sunny. I never should have doubted you. Not even for a second. I knew I'd made a mistake before my plane landed in Dallas. Hell, I knew it before the plane was in the air. I just couldn't admit it to myself."

"Why did you get involved again? Will has his money and his paintings back. You'd done what you promised you would do for him."

"Truthfully?"

"Please, Jake."

"Will pushed me to keep looking. He never believed you were guilty, and I think he knew I didn't believe it, either. He finally pushed hard enough. Siblings can be a pain in the ass."

"I'm beginning to see that."

"Oh shit." He rubbed a hand over his face. "I'm sorry. See, I can't think straight when you're around. Maybe that's why I needed to go home to figure this out."

She dropped her gaze to her mug then used both hands

to spin it in place. "You hurt me, Jake. I thought we had something."

"You weren't wrong," he said, consulting his mug. "I felt it, too. Something." He tipped the mug, examined its contents—like he'd find answers or the right words there. "Did I fuck it up beyond repair, Sunny? Can you forgive me for not believing in you? For not sticking by you?"

"I want to. I really do, but I need time, Jake. This entire thing has made me question everything in my life. And now, I have a sister who apparently hates me and has for some time. It's a lot to process, and until they drop the charges, I'm still the alleged perpetrator of several major crimes."

Hearing the despair in her voice and knowing he was partly responsible for it, twisted his gut up in knots. He'd do anything in his power to bring sunshine back into her life. Rising, he rounded the island. As if her body remembered his, she turned to face him. He stepped into the V of her legs. She tilted her face up, and he gave in to temptation, cradling her cheek with his palm. The pain and uncertainty in her eyes were like arrows to his heart, wounding him.

"I'm so sorry, sweetheart. I never meant for you to get hurt." He stroked her soft skin with his thumb, memorizing the curve of her cheek, then the softness of her lips. "I love you, Sunny. More than you can ever know. I hope you can find it in your heart to forgive me, but if you can't, I'll understand. You deserve a man who won't ever doubt you, one who'll cherish you forever. One who would walk through Hell to protect you." He kissed her forehead then met her gaze. "I want to be that man, Sunny. I swear to God, if you can forgive me, I'll be that man for you."

Footsteps sounded from the hallway. Jake reluctantly stepped away. He caught the sheen of tears in her eyes and cursed himself anew for making her cry.

Her father stepped into the room. "Woke the son of a bitch up. He'll meet us tomorrow morning at my house, look over this new evidence."

The news eased some of Jake's anxiety. "He's willing to

listen, so that's good." Once a cop made up his mind, it wasn't easy to convince him he might be wrong. Jake hoped Detective Reeves was different.

"If he doesn't see what's obvious, we'll go over his head." Mr. Sheldon gave his daughter a hug. "We'll get this cleared up tomorrow. I promise."

"Thanks, Dad. I appreciate you standing by me."

Jake didn't think she meant the comment to be a jab at his lack of faith, but it hit him hard anyway. He turned his back on them while he tried to get his emotions under control. He'd bared his soul, pleaded his case. It was up to Sunny to either forgive him or not. Jake took another sip from his glass. The aged bourbon burned a trail all the way to his stomach.

"I know you, Sunshine. You don't have a dishonest bone in your body, and with your acting skills, you'd never pull off that kind of deceit."

"Hey." Her laugh was sweet music to Jake's ears. "I'm not so bad. Ask Jake. I pulled off quite the performance with the real estate agent we questioned. Tell him, Jake."

Stunned at the easy banter and teasing lilt in her voice, Jake spun around. Her eyes were still bright with unshed tears, but her smile was that of an angel. "Yeah," he croaked. He cleared his throat, shifting his gaze away from her before he forgot he had no right to touch her. "You should have seen her. She pretended to be interested in moving out of the city, got the woman to show us pictures of the place my brother and Jessica asked about. Because she played her part so well, we were able to get the address and verify the new owners weren't Cecil and Jessica."

Mr. Sheldon raised an eyebrow. "Well, well. I guess the apple doesn't fall far from the old tree."

Sunny shook her head. "Old tree? Dad, you aren't very old." Then she shifted her gaze to Jake. "And who says I'm not interested in moving out of the city?"

"Speaking of the city," her dad interrupted before Jake could press Sunny regarding her statement, "it's a lengthy drive. If we want to get any sleep at all tonight, we need to get moving."

Sunny hopped off her barstool. "I'll pack a bag since they haven't released my brownstone yet."

Jake's gaze followed her out of the room. When she was gone, he started grabbing mugs. Her dad's voice gave him pause. "Leave them. We have staff who'll come in tomorrow and clean up."

"Okay. I'll put them in the sink." He also turned off the burner beneath the teakettle.

"I've got plenty of room. You'll stay with us?"

His every thought centered on clearing Sunny's name, and he hadn't even thought of making a hotel reservation. He nodded. "Okay, but you'd better check with Sunny first. I don't want her to be uncomfortable."

The actor clapped him on the back. "Are you blind, son? She's in love with you."

"Oh, no, sir. You're mistaken. I betrayed her." He was rambling but couldn't seem to stop himself. "She has every right to hate me."

"But she doesn't. She was mad at you. Wanted to throw you to the sharks a couple of times, but she doesn't hate you. But make no mistake, if you hurt her again, I'll turn you into fish bait myself." He squeezed Jake's shoulder hard enough to make the younger man wince. "Am I making myself clear?"

Jake swallowed hard. "Yes, sir. Crystal."

He eased up on Jake's shoulder—patted him on the back. "I'm glad we got everything cleared up. Do you like to fish, Jake?" He steered Jake toward the front door where they waited for Sunny. "I've got a boat. She's a beaut. A thirty-seven-footer. Twin inboard motors. We should take her out sometime, you and me. Get to know each other. You ever caught a striped bass?"

"Dad." Sunny came down the stairs, carrying a small overnight bag. "Jake doesn't want to hear your fish stories." She handed Jake her bag then slid her arms into a puffy jacket she'd brought down with her. "If you haven't figured out by now, Dad loves to fish. If you aren't interested, better tell him now, or you'll never shut him up."

"Uh, no, I mean, I like to fish." Leaving her dad to set the alarm and lock up, he followed Sunny out. He dropped her bag next to his in the trunk of her dad's Bentley then climbed into the backseat behind Sunny. He didn't mind riding in the back. This way, he'd have several hours to stare at her. Mr. Sheldon slid behind the wheel. "Did Sunny tell you I live on a lake? I keep a boat at a nearby marina. It's only a twenty-footer, but it's plenty big enough for me. Maybe you could come down sometime. You ever do any lake fishing?"

He talked fishing with her dad until Sunny gave up trying to get a word in and drifted off to sleep. From then on, their conversation revolved around more practical matters.

"How long can you stay?" Mr. Sheldon asked.

Jake didn't take his eyes off the woman sleeping in the front passenger seat. "A few days. I left in a hurry. I'll need to do some work while I'm here then I've got a couple of court cases coming up next week. I have to be back for those."

"Her life is here," her dad stated, unnecessarily.

"I'm aware of the geographical problem. I don't know how we'll make this work, but if it matters as much to her as it does to me, we'll figure it out."

"The media frenzy died down some over the last few weeks. After this news breaks, it'll pick up again. Can you handle the scrutiny?"

Jake caught her dad's gaze on him in the rearview mirror. "I can handle anything your daughter needs me to, sir. I let her down once, I won't do it again."

The actor nodded. "You'll do, Ingram. I think you'll do."

A sleepy voice made them both smile. "Leave him alone, Dad. I'm a grown woman. I can take care of myself."

"Never said you couldn't, Sunshine. Never said you couldn't."

"Her name's Sunshine?"

"Sunshine Margery Sheldon. Margie said Sunny was a ray of sunshine after all the months she'd spent on bedrest.

When they brought around the papers to fill out for her birth certificate, we looked at each other and we both said Sunshine at the same time." He smiled at the memory. "She's been Sunny ever since."

"That's a nice story. They named me after my father. Jacob Tyler Ingram. Tyler was my mother's family name. I've got two younger brothers. We all got the same middle name. They're named after my mother's brothers, William and Richard Tyler." Talking about them reminded him he needed to call Will, fill him in on everything happening here, and to see if Rick had shown up. He checked his phone for the time and decided it was too late to call. He'd check in first thing in the morning. He'd rather wake them both up early than roust them out of a sound sleep in the middle of the night.

"Will is the artist, right? What does Richard do?"

"Rick," Jake corrected then explained about his brother's stint in the Marines before returning home to open his own home remodeling business. By the time he'd finished, they were entering the city. He shut up to let the man concentrate on driving.

Her dad dropped them off in front of his house then parked his car in the garage a few blocks away where he rented space for several vehicles. Sunny unlocked the door then led him inside.

"My room and Dad's room are on the second floor. Guest rooms are on the third floor. Pick whichever you want." She shed her coat, hanging it on a hook on the hall tree behind the door. "Help yourself to anything in the kitchen. Dad's casual about guests. His house is your house." She waved her hand around. "You get the idea." She made for the stairs, overnight bag in hand.

Jake caught up easily, taking her bag in his free hand. "I'll get it." He could see she wanted to argue, but fatigue, or maybe something else, made her reconsider.

"Okay, but, Jake, I haven't made up my mind yet about you. About us. Just so you know."

He nodded. "I know. I won't pressure you, Sunshine."

Using her full name earned him a smile. "Don't call me that. I hate it."

"Why?" He trailed her up the stairs and to a room a much younger Sunny had decorated, judging by the pink frilly curtains and matching comforter that set off the white furniture. Pink flowered wallpaper adorned the walls. Jake's eyes crossed at the overpowering floral pattern.

Sunny stood in the doorway, blocking him from entering, thank God. He didn't know how anyone could spend ten minutes, let alone an entire night, in her room. "Sunshine is a hippy name. Like Moon or River. Clearly, my parents were out of their minds with joy or something else I don't want to think about when they came up with my name."

"Your dad has a perfectly reasonable explanation for your name."

"Yeah, I've heard it. Bullshit, I tell you." She pulled the door halfway closed. "Upstairs, Jake. Take your pick. I'll see you in the morning." She shut the door in his face.

CHAPTER TWENTY-TWO

Sunny clasped her hands in her lap to keep them from shaking. Detective Reeves had been there almost two hours, listening and asking questions, and she'd been a nervous wreck the entire time. She hated someone she'd called a friend for the last five years or so could be so devious. Finding out the person was her half sister only made the deception worse. Sunny didn't want to see her sister go to prison for the possession and sale of stolen merchandise, but she had no intention of serving a sentence for something she didn't do, either.

Her dad called his team, and they were working on a way to spin the story so it didn't sound as bad as it really was. Talk about a Hollywood-style scandal. This took the cake. It was the kind of story even the legitimate news outlets couldn't ignore. She'd lived most of her life in the shadows of the spotlight trained on her dad. Since her arrest, she'd been the one under scrutiny. Once the latest became public, her entire family would be held up to public scorn. A marital affair. An illegitimate child. A high-profile crime. A sibling framing another for said crime. Her mother would be the object of pity. Until they found Ginger/Samantha and got a confession out of her, Sunny would forever be under suspicion by the public, if not the police.

Then there was Jake. Keeping his name out of it would be impossible. The tabloids already linked him to her and ran with the story of their trip upstate, turning it into something lurid, if not illegal. He said he could deal with the fallout, but could he really? Sunny'd seen others who were used to the public scrutiny buckle under the pressure. And what about his law practice? Would his notoriety, even if short-lived, influence his livelihood?

Everywhere she looked, her life spilled over onto those she loved, and not in a good way. Her mom and dad had to put up with her, but Jake didn't. If it all became too much, he could walk away. He'd done it once, and it hurt more than she ever imagined. The man held her heart in his hands, and the thought of him crushing it a second time was the only thing she feared more than going to jail.

Detective Reeves shuffled the pages Jake's PI had provided and stuffed them back in the folder. "Mind if I take these?"

The question jerked Sunny out of her maudlin thoughts.

Jake made a dismissive gesture. "Help yourself."

Everyone stood when the detective did. "Ms. Sheldon, I'll let you know if this information checks out, but Mr. Ingram has put forth a logical scenario to explain many of the unanswered questions in your case."

"So, I'm not off the hook yet?" God, she hated the way her voice shook, but she couldn't help it. She was so cold inside, her whole body trembled with it.

"No, ma'am. Not until I can verify the latest information. Given the photograph of your sister, I can see how she could pass herself off as you. It would be best if we could find her, but if her connection to Cecil Hawthorne checks out, and what her building super said holds, those facts would cast a different light on the investigation but not necessarily rule out your involvement."

Disappointment felt like a giant stone hanging around her neck. The news Jake brought last night gave her hope. Too much hope, according to the detective. Without the confession of one of the real culprits, everything the police had still pointed to Sunny's involvement in some way. All she had in her favor was the testimony of a building superintendent who couldn't say for sure if the paintings he'd helped tote up the stairs were the ones stolen from Hawthorne's gallery.

Even she had to admit, the story about a sister she hadn't known she had, who, for reasons unknown, happened to have it out for her, sounded a bit too convenient. Until the missing sister was found and her motives uncovered, a cloud of suspicion would hover over Sunny's head. Another reason Jake should stay far away from her.

Her dad spoke up. "Samantha has access to her trust fund. Maybe she's using it to fund this caper. She's got to be living on something."

Detective Reeves tucked the folder under his arm. "I'll try to get a warrant for her financials and her phone records. Based on all this"—he tapped the folder—"I would expect the judge to sign off on the warrant. But remember, Hawthorne was paying her rent. If she had the kind of money you say she has, then why wasn't she paying her own rent? I know that neighborhood. No one with a trust fund would live there unless they didn't have a choice."

"You think she's depleted her trust fund?" Mr. Sheldon sounded horrified at the thought.

"Happens more often than you think," the detective said as he ambled toward the front door.

"You'll keep Ms. Sheldon informed?" Jake asked.

The detective opened the door. "Of course, and thanks for running down this new information."

Jake banged a fist on the closed door. "Fuck!"

Sunny sank to the sofa, exhausted from the strain of keeping it together in the presence of the detective, when she wanted to shout and cry, and possibly throw something. She clenched her fists as frustration boiled to the surface, spilling down her cheeks in a torrent. "He doesn't believe me. He thinks Ginger and I did this together and we had a falling out and she left me holding the bag."

Suddenly, Jake was there, wrapping her in his arms, providing a bulwark to protect and support her. "Shh," he whispered as he cradled her head against his shoulder. "It's going to be alright. He'll follow the evidence. Those three must be living on something. It wouldn't take long for three people to blow through the money they stole from Will's accounts, especially if they're still in Manhattan."

"You think they're still in the city?" Glass clinked on glass as Sunny's dad poured himself a drink at the sideboard.

Jake's hands felt wonderful on her, one stroking her hair, the other firm on her back. "I do. At least Samantha is. She went to a lot of trouble to frame Sunny. Stands to reason she'd hang around close enough to watch it all unfold."

"Do you trust the PI you hired?"

Jake shrugged. "A friend I attended law school with recommended him. So far, he's been professional and discreet. Why?"

"Because I have information on Samantha's trust fund. Maybe he could at least tell us if the principle is still intact. I can't believe she could have blown through it in the few years since she gained control of it."

"I take it the principle was substantial." Jake held her tight, his warmth slowly battling the pervasive cold inside.

"If she managed it even halfway right, she could have lived comfortably the rest of her life, even in New York."

Jake whistled low. "Then we need to find out what she's done with it." He bent his head so he could see her face. "You okay?"

Sunny nodded and sniffed as she swiped her damp cheeks with her fingers. "Better." She pushed away from him, instantly regretting the loss of his heat and his strength. "Everything came crashing in all of a sudden." She patted the giant wet spot on his shirt. "Thanks for letting me lean on you."

His smile was like a ray of sunshine aimed right at her heart. "Anytime, sweetheart. Anytime." He used a thumb to brush away an errant tear from her cheek then he looked past her to her dad. "I'll call him. You got the information handy?"

✦✧✦

Jake didn't want to leave her, but he had obligations back home he couldn't shirk, not if he wanted to keep his license to practice law. Sunny sat in the back of the limo her dad hired to take Jake to the airport, looking a little lost and not at all the spirited woman he knew and loved.

He was still getting used to the idea of being in love. It no longer scared him the way it did at first. He didn't have a clue how they could manage to be together, but he was dedicated to finding a way. But first, he needed to take care of things at home, and they had to get the charges dropped against her. Completely clearing her name would be nice, but as long as the real culprits remained at large, she'd remain under suspicion. He didn't want her to live with a dark cloud hanging over her. He vowed to do all he could to change her situation. His PI was working on the information Sunny's dad provided. Hopefully, he'd come up with a solid lead soon. Every day suspicion lay on her shoulders killed a little more of Sunny's spirit.

Framing her face with his hands, he looked deep into her eyes. "I love you. No matter what, don't forget you mean the world to me."

"I love you, too, Jake." Tears, almost ever-present now, leaked from the corner of her eyes. "Do you have to go?"

"Yes, but I'll be back." He thumbed her tears away. "If this doesn't get cleared up soon, you should come stay with me. If Detective Reeves knows where you are, he shouldn't care if you get away for a while."

She sniffed back more tears and a hint of a smile broke across her face. "I'd like to see where you live. And I could see Hank and Melody, too."

"They'd love to have you come visit, but, call me selfish,

I want you all to myself—in my bed.”

Instead of tears, her eyes sparkled then with the same want he felt to his core. “I can't think of anywhere else I want to be.” She dipped her head, resting her forehead on his chest. “I need you. I want this all to go away so we can be together.”

He held her tight, memorizing the feel of her soft body next to his hard one. He'd never felt this all-encompassing love for another person before. He loved his brothers, would do anything for them, but being physically distant from them didn't make him feel like a part of him was missing. “We're going to be together; I promise. We just have a few things to work out first.” Like where they would live. What he would do for a living if he left Texas behind to be with her.

A horn honked as a car sped around them, protesting their prolonged curbside goodbye.

“I've got to go, sweetheart.” He kissed her, pouring the cocktail of emotions swirling inside him into the connection. Showing her without words how she affected him, how much he hated to leave her. When he broke away, he captured her gaze with his. “I'm leaving my heart in your hands. Take care of it until I get back.”

Her bottom lip trembled, and the tears he hated so much were back. Before he changed his mind and tossed his career away, he climbed from the car, carry-on in hand, and walked inside the terminal.

Jake had never spent a more hellish week. Not even when Rick had been in Afghanistan and they hadn't heard from him following an attack on his forward base. Somehow, call it a brother's intuition, he'd known Rick was okay. The tremble in Sunny's voice, the longing in her tone, however, gutted him every damn time. He placed a call to Detective Reeves.

“Mr. Ingram,” the detective said. “If you're calling for an

update, I'm sorry to disappoint you. I'm still waiting on the warrant for Samantha Sheldon's financials and phone records."

Jake shook his head at the delay. He understood the crime they were talking about wasn't murder, but someone's life was still fucked up. A little expediency would be appreciated. He kept his impatience to himself, though, and got to the point of his call. "I'd like Sunny Sheldon to come stay with me in Texas until this is over."

"Does she want to go to Texas?"

"I believe she does. Look, I'm an officer of the court. I'll take full responsibility for her while she's here. I'll even come to New York and escort her to Texas. If you need her back there for anything at any time, I'll escort her home."

Jake listened to the sound of papers shuffling on the other end as the detective considered his request. "Okay, but I want her to surrender her passport, and I'll expect her to report in weekly. She's still a suspect in a high-profile crime, Mr. Ingram."

"I understand, and your terms are fair. Will it be okay if she leaves her passport with her lawyer?"

"That's fine. Have him call me when he has it in hand." A long sigh sounded over the phone. "Between you, me, and a stump, Mr. Ingram, I don't think Sunny had anything to do with any of this. However, the evidence says she's complicit, and I have to follow the evidence."

Jake was thankful the detective shared his thoughts. They went a long way to relieving his fear Sunny would be held responsible for something she didn't do. "I appreciate your candor, Detective. Keep following the evidence, and eventually it will lead you to the truth. Sunny Sheldon is innocent. I wouldn't bring her to the same town my brother lives in if I thought, for a second, she had anything to do with the crime committed against him. And for the record, he doesn't believe she was involved, either. He's the one who has pushed me to investigate on my own. That's how much he believes in her innocence."

"Victims of crimes often see what they want to see, but I'll take your brother's support for Ms. Sheldon under advisement. She's fortunate to have the kind of support she has."

Jake ended the call with a promise to stay in touch then he called Sunny to give her the good news.

CHAPTER TWENTY-THREE

The minute she set foot in Jake's home, her body relaxed. She didn't realize how much the stress she was under was tied to being in the city where her life had gone to hell in the proverbial handbasket until now.

Jake's home was beautiful and welcoming. The wide-open spaces surrounding it, dotted with wide-reaching oak trees, created a relaxed atmosphere she could get addicted to. Like she was addicted to Jake. He'd held her hand on the plane and told her stories about his hometown, some of which she found difficult to believe. But right now, standing in the home he'd built for himself, she'd believe anything he told her. He'd promised to bring her here, and, somehow, he'd made it happen.

"Straight through there is the pool." He pointed to a cased opening off what she'd call a formal living room. "There's a pool house slash guesthouse off to the right. If you follow the path past the pool, it will take you to the lake and the fire pit Will built for his bonfire."

"I want to see it all, Jake, but later, if you don't mind?"

"Sure." He raked his hand through his hair. "You must be exhausted. I've got two guest rooms—"

Sunny stopped him with a finger to his lips. "I don't want to be alone, Jake." She noted the immediate change in his posture and the way his lips curved slightly beneath her finger while his blue eyes darkened with arousal.

"I'm trying to be a polite host," he said.

"I don't want polite, either."

He dropped the one suitcase he'd brought in then circled her waist with his hands. God, she loved having his hands on her.

"What do you want, then?"

"I want to forget the last few months happened. I want you inside me because when you are, I can't think of anything else but the way you make me feel."

He placed one hand on her hip where he tugged, bringing her up against him. The other hand roamed up to cup her breast, kneading until she moaned and reached between them to touch his shaft. "If I have one goal while you're here, sweetheart, it's to make sure the only thing you think about is us. Together."

"This is a good start."

"You sure you don't want to rest first? I can wait." The action of his roaming hands to the contrary.

"I'll have plenty of time to rest later." She went up on tiptoes, wrapped her free hand around his nape, and dragged him down for a kiss. As she'd hoped, their lips touching was like tossing a match at a gas can. Semi-polite touching ignited into a blaze that heated them from the inside out. She'd worn leggings and an oversized sweater for the plane ride. In seconds, the sweater was on the floor and her back hit the cold wall of the entryway.

"God, I've missed you. Missed this," he growled as he yanked her bra down, exposing one breast to his gaze. Using his thumb, he teased the nipple to a hard point. Sunny wrapped both arms around his head, encouraging him to take what he wanted. He didn't disappoint. Like a man starved, he opened his mouth over her and sucked. Sunny groaned and tightened her grip on his head as bolts of lightning shot from her tit to her core. Her hips moved of their own accord, seeking the intimate connection she'd missed for too long.

Jake wedged a knee between her legs, bringing it up until she rode his thigh. The friction, the blessed pressure felt good, but she needed more.

"Jake, please," she begged.

His slipped his free hand beneath the waistband of her pants, right to her aching core. She gasped as his fingers explored her folds then found what they sought. He tugged hard on her nipple at the same time he drove his fingers deep inside her dripping channel. Sunny cried out as she came, her body jerking and clutching, quaking. He showed no mercy, ravishing her breast and finger-fucking her until her arms dropped from his head and she sagged against him like a worn-out dishrag.

He removed his hand from her gently then, oh so tenderly, tugged her bra cup up to cover her swollen breast. Sunny dropped her forehead to his chest. She inhaled deeply, reveling in the familiar smell of him she'd come to associate with home. "I'm sorry."

Jake lifted her into his arms as if she weighed nothing then carried her down a hallway. "Nothing to be sorry for, sweetheart. You had a lot of pent-up stress."

The smile in his voice reassured her. "What about you?"

"I've been managing my stress on my own. I'll live a few hours more." Images of him providing his own stress relief flitted through her brain, making her core throb. He entered a bedroom. His, she'd guess by the size of the bed he carefully set her down upon. Jake dropped to one knee and carefully removed her ankle boots and socks. He kissed one foot then the other before rising to his feet. "Lay back."

Sunny did as requested then lifted her hips, allowing him to strip the leggings from her body. She didn't argue as he tucked her in then closed the drapes over the sliding door, artificially darkening the room.

"No arguments," he said, placing a chaste kiss on her forehead. "Rest. You're going to need your strength because you're right. I, too, have a lot of pent-up stress, the kind only being with you can alleviate."

She wanted to argue, but the soft bed, and the dark room, and, yes, the warm glow inside from the orgasm made her eyelids heavy. She might have been asleep before he left the room.

೭ఞ

Leaving her half naked in his bed might have been the hardest thing Jake had ever done in his life. Harder than all the times he'd walked away from her in New York combined, and each one of those had been harder than the previous one. The last time nearly killed him. He'd damn near said fuck it to his career and followed her back to her dad's house.

If he had, she wouldn't be here now, and as he tried to tame his urge to wake her and fuck her into next week, he couldn't shake the feeling she belonged right where she was. In his house. In his bed. *His* being the operative word. He'd see how she felt about it after she had a chance to rest and decompress from the stress she'd been under for the last few months.

There wasn't much for her in Willowbrook besides him, and he wasn't vain enough to think he was enough for a woman like her. She was used to a vibrant life in the art world, in Manhattan, no less. Compared to the Big Apple, Willowbrook might as well be on Mars. There was zero to do here.

Jake grabbed a beer from the fridge then propped his feet up on the coffee table in his den. Staring at the black screen on the TV, he tried to envision himself living in Manhattan and couldn't do it. The noise, the dirty streets, the towering buildings. It made him claustrophobic thinking about it. Sunny hinted she might be amiable to living outside the city. From what he'd seen of Long Island, which, granted, wasn't much, he might be okay out there, but he couldn't afford any of the homes he'd seen. The places they'd explored upstate weren't bad. Some of the scenery had been downright gorgeous, but Jake had little or no experience with winter. Not the kind they had there with snow that stayed for months and had to be plowed from the roads.

He had to face it; Texas was home for him. Maybe he'd ask Will what he thought. He'd lived in Manhattan for years and survived. Barely. Three urban vipers had nearly done him in, but he'd gotten out, come home, and survived.

So, maybe Will wasn't the best person to ask.

He was getting ahead of himself. Sunny'd been here for less than an hour, and he was already looking for reasons for her not to fall in love with Texas. She had friends here. He couldn't recall her mentioning a single friend in Manhattan. Was that the way people lived there? Isolated in their home and insulated by their jobs? Alone yet surrounded by masses of humans all so busy living they didn't have a life.

Having finished off his beer, he returned to the fridge for another one then stopped to peer out at the pool. He'd turned the heater on a few weeks ago, and a foggy mist rose from the surface now, shrouding the water from view. Jake set his beer down then opened the door. Stepping out into the cool fall air, he stripped down to his boxers and dove into the deep end of the pool. The water was warm compared to the outside air, and as his head broke the surface in the shallow end, he drew in a lungful of bracing air then dove under to swim to deeper water. He kept up a grueling pace, swimming beneath the surface rather than on top to avoid the cooler air and because it took more energy to swim underwater.

Maybe, if he tired himself out, he'd be able to sleep, too. The last week had taken a physical toll on him. Between three court appearances and missing Sunny in every way possible, he'd practically given up on sleep. He'd cleared his calendar for the next week, intending to spend his time with Sunny, in and out of bed. He wanted her to really see Willowbrook. And he wanted her to see him. See the real Jake Ingram. See where he'd come from. Humble beginnings compared to her. Humble, middle, and end as well. There wasn't anything fancy about him. Other than a dream of being an author someday, his dreams were simple ones. He wanted his brothers to be happy, and, despite his discontent with his business, he liked helping people.

Maybe he did need a change. Maybe he could be happy in New York.

He broke the surface again, gasping for air. He shook his head, sending water arcing out across the pool. His hair follicles tingled, signaling a change in the atmosphere. He spun around and wiped his eyes. Sunny stood at the edge of the pool, one of his shirts wrapped tight around her. Her feet were bare, one tucked on top of the other. She looked like she was freezing, and he'd never seen anything more alluring in his life.

"Jake?"

He stroked to the shallow end, stood, letting the water cascade down his body. The frigid air did nothing to ease the state of his arousal. She did that to him, every fucking time he saw her. "Sunny. Did you need something, sweetheart?"

She wiped at her eyes with the heel of one hand while holding his shirt closed with the other. "I woke up and wondered where you were."

"Right here." He put his foot on the lowest step, going to her. "Can I get you anything?"

"I-I need you, Jake. Please?"

He reached the top step. "Come on, let me take you back to bed."

She shook her head. "Is the water warm?"

He glanced at the mist rising from the water. "It's not bad. Want to give it a try?"

Up close, he could still see the fatigue ringing her eyes, but there was a spark buried deep inside. "If you'll hold me. I'm so cold inside, Jake. I need you to hold me, make me warm again."

Jake swallowed past the lump in his throat. His heart jackhammered against his ribs. He reached for the collar of his shirt, tugged it to expose her bare shoulders. "Anything you want, sweetheart."

She shivered, and he placed a kiss in the crook where her neck and shoulder met. She smelled like sunshine and some sweet essence he identified with her and her alone.

"I want you. Always you."

He skimmed his hands down her arms until the shirt gave way, leaving her naked before him. Mist swirled around her ankles and the landscape lights highlighted the curves of her body and glinted off the moisture in her eyes. The truth hit him like a sledgehammer to the knees. He'd live anywhere she wanted. Do anything to be worthy of the trust she gave him so freely. Lacing his fingers through hers, he shuffled backward, tugging her along with him until she stood shoulder-deep in the warm water. Only then did he take her in his arms and confess all to her. "You'll always have me. Always."

Sunny draped her arms over his shoulders and, with a little bounce, wrapped the rest of her body around his. He walked them farther in until the water skimmed his shoulders then he lifted her slightly and entered her, sealing his pledge with his body.

"Jake." His name was a sacred whisper she wrote on his heart as her body rose and fell on his, the water rippling between them, caressing, and washing the past away.

"Sunshine," he whispered as he gazed into her eyes. "Don't ever leave me."

Jewels danced from her wet hair as she shook her head. "I won't. I can't. I only feel whole when you're inside me."

He was a goner. Drowning in her words. Drowning in her. She stole his breath just as she'd stolen his heart. "Marry me, Sunny. Tomorrow. Hell, tonight. I know people. I can make it happen."

"Okay. But not tonight. I want to feel you inside me all night, Jake. I need you."

"Your wish is my command, Sunshine."

EPILOGUE

Three months later…

Sunny stood before the full-length mirror in the bride's chamber of the church the Ingram's had belonged to for as long as anyone could recall. "I can't believe this is finally happening."

Melody, her closest friend and Matron of Honor, sighed. "Believe it, girlfriend. Hank came up a few minutes ago to tell me Jake is pacing a bare spot in the carpet, waiting for you."

"Oh no!"

"No worries. He's a nervous groom, is all. Hank said he was afraid you'd come to your senses and run."

"I came to my senses when I agreed to marry him. Best decision of my life."

Mel flounced the cathedral-length veil, allowing it to float to the floor in a wide arc of lace-edged tulle. "You're gorgeous, Sunny. Your mother's dress is timeless and stunning."

"I'm so happy." She used the blue antique hanky Melody had loaned her for the occasion to dab at the tears that lurked right below the surface these days. "I don't deserve a man like Jake."

"Shut up." Mel grabbed a tissue and helped dry her

friend's tears. "He's a lucky man to be getting a woman like you, and he knows it. Now, take a deep breath, and let's get this show on the road."

Sunny laughed through the relentless tears. At least they were happy tears. She had so much to be grateful for. She'd been all set to marry Jake, had been on the way to see the Justice of the Peace three months ago when the call came for her to return to New York. They'd found her sister and her two cohorts in a rented house in Brooklyn. Cecil Hawthorne and Jessica Blackwell had covered their tracks well, but Samantha had left a paper trail leading directly to the place where the threesome, yes, threesome, had been living since they'd pulled off the caper. The money they'd stolen had run out fast, and they'd begun dipping into Samantha's trust fund.

Her sister admitted to planting the paintings and selling the one to a customer who had no prior purchase record with the gallery. All because she believed Sunny had the life she should have had. Sunny still didn't understand why her father hadn't played a part in Samantha's life. Seemed to her, once the secret was out and his marriage over, there was no reason not to acknowledge his other daughter. But it wasn't her problem to figure out.

"My dad's down there?"

"He is, and your mother. I think it's special to have both walk you down the aisle."

Sunny spun on her heels. "Oh, Melody, I'm so sorry. This must be so hard for you." Melody's father, Earl Ravenswood, a legendary rock star, had died on her tenth birthday. Since the circumstances of his death came to light, Melody had a rocky relationship with her mother. "I didn't think…"

"No worries. I'm over it. Hank and I had a beautiful wedding, and you will, too. So, dry those eyes, that's an order, and let's get out there before Jake comes barreling in here and drags you to the altar himself."

"He'd do it, too. You should have seen how upset he was when we didn't make it to the JP as planned. Getting him to wait, given the circumstances"—she placed a loving hand over her belly—"was nearly impossible."

"I heard all about it, multiple times." Mel gathered up the train and veil worthy of a Hollywood wedding, which it had starred in once upon a time. "Jake has made no secret of his impatience. I really think he's afraid you'll wise up and run."

"Never. Jake is all I've ever wanted, and more. I can't wait to be his wife, and the mother of his children. Nothing has ever felt more right."

MacKenzie barreled in carrying three bouquets. "You'd better hurry. Jake is not a patient groom. If you don't show soon, we'll have to sedate him." She passed out the flowers, one for Sunny, one for Melody, and kept one for herself. She held Sunny's billowing skirt to one side so Melody could get past. "Everybody ready?"

"Ready," Melody said.

"Ready," Sunny chimed in.

"Okay, let's get you married." Kenzie practically shoved the Matron of Honor out the door then followed, turning halfway down the hallway to make sure Sunny hadn't bolted.

Sunny paused in the doorway leading to the narthex. Her mother, looking radiant in a blue gown in a color similar to the bride's maids' dresses, rushed forward. "Sunshine, you are breathtaking. My dress looks better on you than it did on me."

"Oh, I wouldn't say that." Her dad, looking like the dazzling star he was in his custom tuxedo, beamed at his ex-wife, the woman he still claimed to be the love of his life. "You took my breath away on our wedding day, and you still do." Sunny noted the wistful look in his eyes just before he turned to watch her enter the room. "You're glowing, Sunshine. Jake's knees are going to buckle when he sees you."

She took his arm then her mother's. "You think so, Dad?"

"If they don't, I'll knock them out from under him myself."

"Dad," she mock scolded. "Be nice."

"Hey, he's marrying my daughter. I have every right to question his worthiness."

"No need to worry," Sunny said as they reached the door, and she caught sight of Jake and his brothers waiting at the front of the church.

Melody had let her in on a secret. Around town, the Ingram brothers were known as the brothers grim as in ghastly, gloomy, and glum. Many single women over the years had tried unsuccessfully to crack through the hard shells. Then MacKenzie had won Will's heart. And now, Sunny was about to marry the eldest of the bunch, leaving the youngest, Rick, the last single brother. She'd gotten to know him since she'd moved to Willowbrook, and she had a hunch he might not be as available as everyone thought. Only time would tell. Until then…

"Jake's a wonderful man, Dad." It was a truth written on her heart. He was loyal to those he loved. He hadn't betrayed her. He'd been showing his loyalty to his brother. The man who now had a steadying hand on Jake's shoulder. Alone, each of the brothers turned heads, but together, lord have mercy. They were a sight to behold.

She felt for those who'd tried and failed to capture the attention of one of the brothers. They were a brooding lot, but once they gave their heart, they did it without reservation.

Melody wished her luck then walked regally down the aisle to an original tune composed by her husband and played softly by his band, BlackWing. They'd taken several weeks off from their American tour around the holidays and had insisted on being a part of the ceremony. Sunny would have been happy with piped-in music as long as she was marrying Jake today, but they'd offered, and she'd accepted. Who could say they'd had a world-famous rock band play them down the aisle at their wedding?

Next in line, MacKenzie gave her one last, *don't you dare run* look then followed Melody to the altar.

The music shifted to the traditional "Here Comes the

Bride," and Jake turned to face the back of the church. Their gazes met over the sea of heads, and his smile nearly knocked her over with its intensity. His body swayed, and he gripped the altar rail to steady himself.

"Guess I won't have to knock him on his ass after all." Curtis smiled at his daughter then, with his ex-wife, led Sunny down the aisle where her future awaited her.

❧ᵹᴏ

Jake Ingram tugged at the collar of his tuxedo shirt, silently praying his bride hadn't come to her senses and run. He wouldn't blame her if she had, but God, how he hoped she hadn't. As glad as he was to have her name cleared and all charges against her dropped, the timing couldn't have been worse. They'd been minutes from the JP's office where he planned to seal the deal before she could change her mind. Then the call had come, and he'd had to wait three interminably long months to make her his.

In the meantime, he'd learned he was going to be a father. Talk about a sledgehammer to the frontal lobe. Who knew stress could mess with a woman's hormones and screw with the effectiveness of the pill? He couldn't have cared less about how the pregnancy came about. The baby only tied her closer to him, a lifetime bond even more sacred than the one they would make today. He didn't know squat about being a husband or a father. His only role model, his own dad, had been abysmal at both. A good thing, Sunny insisted. All he had to do was ask himself what his dad would have done then do the opposite. *Not terrible advice.*

He was about a breath away from going in search of her when Will placed a hand on his shoulder. He looked up in time to see Melody Travis make her way down the aisle. Will's girlfriend, MacKenzie Carlysle followed. Then the love of his life stood at the back of the church, her father on one side, her mother on the other.

God, she was beautiful. Radiant. Glowing from within.

Her dress was pretty, too. Her mother's, he recalled her saying. But who the hell cared? He would have married her even if she'd worn a tote-sack.

Relief, pride, and the ever-present desire where she was concerned coursed through his body like a potent cocktail. One second, he was smiling at her then, the next, his knees turned to jelly. He reached for the altar rail at the same time Will and Rick grabbed his arms, setting him upright. He shrugged the laughing loons off and straightened. Determined to make it through the ceremony with as much dignity as he could muster. She deserved her special day. Deserved a hell of a lot more than him, but in a few minutes, provided she didn't bolt, she'd be stuck with him for life.

What a life it would be. Once she saw the town, she'd fallen in love with Willowbrook and decided right away it was missing one thing—an art gallery. After their honeymoon, she planned to open the new Sunnyside Gallery in a vacant storefront on Main Street. She'd already convinced Will to let her be the exclusive purveyor of original William H. Ingram paintings and planned to comb the region for other local artists to showcase.

While moving in, she'd found his stash of manuscripts beneath the bed, and, being the nosy person she was, she'd read them then convinced him to let her dad read them. When Jake returned from the honeymoon, he'd be turning over most of his law practice to a junior lawyer he'd hired out of his old firm in Houston. Jake would keep a few clients, like his brothers, then spend the rest of his time writing.

She'd walked into his life, tossed it upside down, shook it a couple of times, and set him on a new path. One he'd gladly walk with her by his side.

She paused briefly at the last row of pews. Raised her gaze to his. And he knew the only place she was going was with him. Hank and his band, BlackWing, struck up Wagner's "Bridal Chorus." The audience rose to watch the bride come down the aisle. Jake couldn't wait another second. Wedding etiquette be damned. He walked to the front row of seats and held out his hand. If he had hold of her hand, he'd have a fighting chance of stopping her before she could get away.

The next few minutes were a blur of promises and declarations. Nothing they hadn't said to each other in private, except, this time, with a lot less clothes between them. He placed a ring on her finger, repeating the words that, until this day, had meant little to him, officially claiming her as his. Then she slid a simple gold band on his finger, and once again, his knees failed him. He reached for her, and she grasped his arm to steady him.

Her words rang in his ears like the clearest bell. "With this ring, I thee wed. For better or for worse. For richer or poorer. In sickness and in health. Until death we do part."

Needing to see her, he lifted his gaze to hers and said the first thing that came to mind. "Yours."

Her cheeks bloomed prettier than cherry blossoms. She dipped her chin, glanced up at him through her lashes, and gave him the vow he'd treasure the most. "Yours."

ABOUT THE AUTHOR

USA Today Best-Selling author Roz Lee is the author of over thirty romances. The first, The Lust Boat, was born of an idea acquired while on a Caribbean cruise with her family, and soon blossomed into a five-book series originally published by Red Sage. Following her love of baseball, Roz turned her attention to sexy athletes in tight pants, writing the critically acclaimed Mustangs Baseball series.

Roz has been married to her best friend, and high school sweetheart, for over four decades. They have two daughters and are the proud grandparents of three adorable grandkids. Roz and her husband live in the wilds of New Jersey with their Labrador Retriever, Bud which is code for Big Unruly Dog.

Even though Roz has lived on both coasts, her heart lies in between, in Texas. A Texan by birth, she can trace her family back to the Republic of Texas. With roots that deep, she says, "You can't ever really leave."

When Roz isn't writing, she's reading or traipsing around the country on one adventure or another. No trip is too small, no tourist trap too cheesy, and no road unworthy of travel.

Learn more at WWW.RozLee.net

9 781966 224105